Helen Dunmore

Helen Dunmore is a full-time writer, who lives in Bristol with her family. Most days she goes to write in an eighth-floor flat where there are no distractions apart from the view. She also loves travelling. Her books have won a number of awards and been translated into thirteen languages.

Contents

Short Stories by

Helen Dunmore

ALiENS DON'T EAT BACON SANDWICHES

mammoth

This collection first published in Great Britain 2000
by Mammoth, an imprint of Egmont Children's Books Limited
239 Kensington High Street, London W8 6SA

Hannah's Tree-house copyright © 2000 Helen Dunmore
The Airman's Sixpence copyright © 1997 Helen Dunmore
First published in *Incredibly Creepy Stories* edited by Tony Bradman,
published by Transworld
The Old Team copyright © 1999 Helen Dunmore
First published in *Family Tree* edited by Miriam Hodgson, Mammoth
The Mars Ark copyright © 1993 Helen Dunmore
First published in *S. F. Stories (tape)* edited by Tony Bradman, published
by HarperCollins
Clyde's Leopard copyright © 1998 Helen Dunmore
First published in Cambridge Readers, Cambridge University Press
Wolf Weather copyright © 1996 Helen Dunmore
First published by Robinson Publishing
Great-grandma's Dancing Dress copyright © 1998 Helen Dunmore
First published in Cambridge Readers, Cambridge University Press
A Gap in the Dark copyright © 1994 Helen Dunmore
First published in *Amazing Adventure Stories* edited by Tony Bradman,
published by Transworld
Aliens Don't Eat Bacon Sandwiches copyright © 1992 Helen Dunmore
First published by Transworld
A Close Match copyright © 1998 Helen Dunmore
First published in *Sisters* edited by Miriam Hodgson, Mammoth
The Golden Gate copyright © 1993 Helen Dunmore
First published in *Mystery Stories (tape)* edited by Tony Bradman, published
by HarperCollins
This collection copyright © 2000 Mammoth
ISBN 0 7497 3861 8
10 9 8 7 6 5 4 3 2 1
A CIP catalogue record for this title is available from the British Library
Typeset by Avon Dataset Ltd, Bidford on Avon, Warwickshire B50 4JH
Printed in Great Britain by Cox & Wyman Ltd, Reading, Berkshire

Contents

Hannah's Tree-house

Mum doesn't like it when I talk about the time she was in hospital.

'Six weeks,' she says. 'It was awful. You must have thought I was never coming home.'

But I always knew she was coming home. Nan had told me she was, and I believed everything Nan said. Nan had never once told me a lie. If you think back to when you were little, it's surprising how many people did tell you lies. Sometimes it was to keep you happy, sometimes it was to make things easier for them.

'Your rabbit's in heaven, eating carrots all day long.'

'You look wonderful in that pink and purple striped T-shirt!'

'Yes, I'll definitely take you to Disneyland . . . when you're a bit older.'

Hmm. I'd rather have the truth, even if it's tough. Then you know where you are. Even the hardest things – like the truth about what happened to Hannah . . .

You don't know about Hannah yet, and nor did I then. It

was the first morning after I'd come to stay at Nan's. I woke up at half-past five. Everything was strange, and I think the noise of the birds woke me. Besides, I had a plan. I used to share Nan's bedroom when I stayed with her, in a camp-bed under the window. Nan was still fast asleep. I tiptoed out of bed, pulled on a sweatshirt, and very gently opened the door so it wouldn't click. I didn't bother about finding my trainers. It was summer.

I held my breath as I tiptoed around the side of the house. I put one bare foot on the grass, then the other. The grass was long and cold and wet. In the tree the birds sang their early songs, and I crept forward, watching them watching me, and not flying away. They weren't frightened at all. Now I know that the reason the birds weren't frightened was that hardly anyone ever came into the garden, but then I thought it was magic.

I was in the garden. I was really in the garden, walking on Mr Barenstein's grass. I could still hear Nan's voice in my head. 'Now, Tara, you are *not* to go in the garden. It belongs to Mr Barenstein, because he has the garden flat. And he's old and tired and he doesn't want any children in there running and shouting.'

But I wasn't running, and I wasn't shouting. I wasn't disturbing anyone, not even the birds. I glanced back at the house, but all the curtains were still closed. Everybody in the three flats was asleep, and I was going to explore all the way to the bottom of the garden. I tiptoed on, and the birds sang at me, warning me. I was on their territory, but I didn't understand that then.

And then I heard a sound. I remember how I flushed all over with terror, in a way that doesn't happen after you're ten years old. I turned, and I saw a window slide up, slowly, creakily. It was Mr Barenstein's window. He'd seen me. He was going to lean out of the window and yell at me so that everyone in the whole house heard. He was going to shout 'WHAT ARE YOU DOING IN MY GARDEN?'

The window slid right up, and Mr Barenstein leaned out. He looked straight at me, and at the long trail of wet footprints I'd left in the grass. I felt as if he'd caught me stealing from him. I wanted to shut my eyes and sink right down into the wet grass and hide there, curled up, and never come out. But I didn't move, and Mr Barenstein didn't shout. Instead he called to me, 'Good morning, little girl!'

Mr Barenstein had never spoken to me before. I'd see him in the hall sometimes, disappearing into his garden flat, his back bowed in its black coat. Once I'd seen him carrying a bunch of white flowers. White flowers, black coat. He had white, wiry hair, and deep-brown eyes that hid under his brows and did not look at me when he passed me in the hall. But he was looking at me now.

'How are you this morning, little girl?' asked Mr Barenstein.

Suddenly I got angry. Why did he keep calling me 'little girl'? He knew my name perfectly well. He lived in the same house as Nan, and he'd seen me hundreds of times.

'My name's Tara,' I said.

'Tara,' said Mr Barenstein. 'Tara. Of course.' He still didn't sound angry, but any minute now I knew he was going to start to shout.

'So,' said Mr Barenstein, 'what are you doing in my garden, Tara?'

I felt ashamed, like a thief, but I felt angry too, because I knew I was not a thief. Why should he try to make me into one?

'I'm not doing anything wrong. I'm not picking flowers or anything,' I said.

'So what *are* you doing?'

I looked back at the line of my footsteps on the wet grass. They looked purposeful, as if my footsteps knew something I did not. I'm exploring, I thought, but I didn't say it.

'You like gardens?' asked Mr Barenstein.

'*Everybody* likes gardens,' I said. 'Except –' Did I dare to say it? Yes, I thought, I will say it. I'm never going to be allowed in the garden again, anyway. Here I was outside with the birds and sun and long grass, and I would never be here again. 'Except you,' I said to Mr Barenstein. 'You *never* go in the garden. Every time I come to Nan's I look out of the window, and I never see you. *Never*. Not even when it's the middle of summer!'

I wanted to say so much more. I wanted to ask Mr Barenstein why he wasted the summer and the garden, while everyone else stared out of their windows and longed to sit in the shade under the tree, or wander barefoot through the soft, cool, grass. I wanted to say, 'If you don't like it, give it to us!' But I didn't.

Mr Barenstein's face crinkled up. Now the shouting was really going to start. But the noise that came out of his mouth was laughter, rusty old laughter that sounded as if he hadn't used it for a long time. Mr Barenstein laughed and laughed.

And I ran. I raced across the wet grass and round the side of the house, and through the front door and up the stairs to the door of Nan's flat. I leaned against the inside of the door, panting. He was going to tell Nan, I knew he was. And Nan would be so angry, and it would spoil everything.

'I want to go home,' I told myself, but I knew I couldn't go home, so I crept back into Nan's bedroom. Nan was still asleep. There was my suitcase on the floor. I hadn't even unpacked it yet. Nan's clock ticked in the corner of the bedroom. *Six weeks*, it said. *Ha ha. Six weeks, six weeks. You've got to stay here for six whole weeks, until your mum's out of hospital.*

'Shut up,' I said to the clock, but quietly, so it wouldn't

wake Nan. *Why* did Mr Barenstein get the garden, and not Nan or Mr and Mrs Giovanni? It was so unfair.

Four days later the sun still shone, and the sky was a clear, perfect blue. I stared out of the window at the garden, and thought about paddling pools and picnics and running on the cool green grass.

'Please, *please*, Nan, can't I go in the garden? Just for five minutes? Mr Barenstein won't know. He's gone to the shops, I saw him.'

'No, Tara,' Nan said. 'Mr Barenstein is old and tired. He needs his peace. He's a good man.'

The sun shone on the grass and shadows flickered under the tree.

'I wish I could go to school,' I said, because it was the worst thing I could think of saying.

'My life!' said Nan. 'I thought you didn't like school.'

I kicked the wall, just a little bit. I liked Nan. I *loved* Nan. But six whole weeks in Nan's flat was a long, long time. And all because Mum was having a baby and her blood pressure was too high. Mum had to stay in hospital until the baby was born. My dad was working on an oil rig. He was saving up his leave to come home and look after Mum and me when the baby was born, and she was out of hospital. Our house was shut and locked and empty.

I was missing everything. The school holidays hadn't

started yet, and it was the best part of term. Sports Day was coming, and the school fair, and the swimming gala. I missed Jasmine, who was my best friend then. I missed Billy, next door's dog. Usually I took him for a walk every day, after school. He was fat, and he puffed. I had to encourage him to walk all the way to the park, because it was good for him. He didn't really walk, he waddled. He was always hoping I was going to carry him, but I had to be stern. 'No, Billy! If you don't walk you'll get so fat you'll die!'

I never let myself think about missing Mum. I was used to Dad being away, but Mum had always been there. She phoned me at Nan's every night, when the phone trolley was brought round to her bed. At the end of the call she would always say, 'I love you,' and I'd say, 'I love you too,' and she'd say, 'I love you three,' and then we'd go on making up higher and higher numbers until Mum said, 'I'd better go now. Someone else wants the phone.' She would always stay on the line until I'd put the phone down. Sometimes I'd wait, to see if she would put it down first, but she never did.

I kicked the wall again. I knew everything would feel quite different if I could go into the garden. Then the phone rang, and I heard Nan's feet hurrying to answer it. But it was much too early for Mum. I listened to the buzz of Nan's voice, but I couldn't hear the words. The phone clicked, and then Nan was standing in the doorway.

'Tara,' Nan said, 'you've been in that garden, haven't you?'

My heart thumped. I knew straight away what had happened. Mr Barenstein had phoned Nan and told her about finding me in his garden. But Nan didn't seem angry.

'I've got a surprise for you,' she said. 'That was Mr Barenstein on the phone. He says if you're so keen on the garden, you can do a bit of work tidying up for him out there. You can dig up the weeds in the flower-beds. He's going to leave some gardening tools outside the back door.'

'I don't even know what weeds look like,' I said. I was so surprised I couldn't be grateful.

'They're all weeds in that garden,' said Nan. 'If it's not grass, it's a weed. You just keep on digging them up, then throw them on a heap.'

I kept on digging. My arms ached, and I was hot, but I liked the smell of the earth when I dug into it with Mr Barenstein's trowel. I kept finding things. There were pieces of broken china, old coins, and rusty bits of metal. I put them all together, to clean them later, in case any of them were valuable. I piled the weeds on to a heap in the corner of the garden, not far from the pear tree. Even though this was the first time I'd been in the garden properly, I felt I knew that pear tree. I'd watched it out of the window so often that I knew all its different moods. When the wind blew the leaves shook and shone. At night they made sharp, black, shadows. In spring the pear tree was covered with white flowers, in summer it had long shiny green leaves, and in autumn the pears grew fatter and fatter until they dropped off the tree. Nobody ever picked them. They rotted on the ground, and the birds pecked at the ones that clung to the branches. Nan said it was a wicked waste.

I knelt on the freshly dug soil, and stared up into the pear tree. I longed to climb it. I'd worked out exactly where I'd put my feet, where I'd swing my legs, where I'd hold on. But I didn't dare. What if Mr Barenstein saw me, and told me to get out of his garden and never come back?

Little by little, a patch of clean brown earth had appeared where I'd dug. It was soft and crumbly and moist. It looked as if it couldn't wait to start growing flowers and vegetables. I wanted to make the patch bigger, so I set to work again. Some of the weeds had long, wriggling roots that went so deep that I had to pull with all my strength to get them out. It was like a battle, but I was winning.

The next morning I got up early, to do some weeding before breakfast. When I ran to find the gardening tools, I saw a brown paper bag propped beside the little fork. On the bag was written in big, black letters: TARA. I pulled it open. Inside, there were two thin rustling packets. I tipped them out. They had bright pictures on them, and planting instructions on the back. One packet was flowers, one was radishes. The flowers were called candytuft. With the seeds there was a little note. PLANT ME, it said.

'Plant me,' I said aloud. I looked at the brown patch of earth I'd cleared the day before, then I turned the packets over to read the instructions. There were little diagrams, too, showing exactly how to plant the seeds.

I raked the soil until it was fine and crumbly, then I found a stick and made little rows. In the bottom of the rows I planted the radish seeds, which looked like tiny peppercorns. I thought the flowers would look better if they were scattered around the radishes, rather than growing in rows next to them. In the picture, the candytuft made thick cushions of colour. I scattered the seeds and crumbled earth over them until they were hidden.

The next morning, there was no brown paper bag. Instead, there was a little green watering-can with a note taped on to it. WATER ME, it said. I knew there was a tap on the outside wall, where Mr Giovanni fixed his hose to wash his car. Mr Giovanni lived in the other flat with Mrs Giovanni, and he was a carpenter. Most of the time he made shelves and fitted cupboards for people's kitchens, but he could make furniture too. When I was about two, he had given me a little chair he'd made.

I filled the watering-can, and went back to the tap again and again until all the soil was dark with moisture. I'd already decided not to say anything to Nan about the seeds. It would be a surprise for her. I planned to arrange some radishes on a plate for her, and fill her little crystal vase with candytuft.

I kept working all morning, clearing as much of the old flower-beds as I could. They were all covered with weeds. The pile of weeds in the corner was huge now, and yesterday's weeds were beginning to wilt. Nan came out with drinks for me, but she didn't stay in the garden. She thought Mr Barenstein might not like it.

'He likes his peace and quiet,' she repeated, and then she went back indoors. Every so often she tapped on the window and waved, and I waved back.

Every day that week I worked in the garden. The sun shone and the seeds needed lots of water. Bit by bit, the tangled, weedy flower-beds were changing into smooth brown earth. The wind blew and the blackbirds sang as they snapped up the worms in the fresh earth. I thought that the garden was the most beautiful place in the world.

'I've nearly finished the big flower-bed!' I told Nan. 'I wish I could live out here all the time.'

'Until it rains,' said Nan.

But the next morning, when I ran out early into the garden, there was another note propped up by the tools. TARA it said on the outside. I unfolded it, wondering what the next surprise was going to be. But all I saw were big black letters that said DON'T COME IN THE GARDEN TODAY.

It was worse than the time when I'd first gone into the

garden, and Mr Barenstein had caught me. My eyes stung, and the words dazzled in front of me. Mr Barenstein didn't like the work I was doing. He wasn't pleased at all. He didn't want me in the garden any more. I crushed the note in my hand, and ran indoors and into Nan's bedroom, and shut the door. I lay down on Nan's big bed. I wasn't going to cry about Mr Barenstein's stupid garden.

'He can do all the work himself. I don't care!' I said to the pillow.

Nan knocked on the door. 'What's wrong, Tara? I thought you were in the garden.'

'I hate the garden. Mr Barenstein says I can't go in there ever again.'

'Did he say that to you?'

'He left a note.' I held out the crumpled note, and Nan read it.

'Maybe he'll let you in the garden tomorrow,' she said. 'Maybe he's ill today and wants some quiet.'

'I don't make a noise. I work!'

'I know, Tara. I know. Listen. What if we go to the swimming-pool today? We can take a picnic and have a day out. You like that.'

'OK.' But I didn't want a picnic. All I wanted was what Mr Barenstein had taken away. I thought of the radishes pushing up shoots without me, and the candytuft unfurling their flowers.

Nan didn't seem to want to go home. I swam and sunbathed, swam and sunbathed, while Nan read her newspaper in the shade. After our picnic Nan suggested the cinema, then burger and chips. We sat for a long time, eating and talking, and it was dark when we got home. Mum rang soon after we got in. She'd been trying all evening, where had we been? I told her about the swimming-pool and the cinema, and the burgers, but nothing about Mr Barenstein stopping me from going into the garden. Mum was glad, because I was having such a good time.

I was very tired, but I couldn't sleep. I kept thinking about the next day, and not being able to go into the garden. I still couldn't work out what I'd done wrong. Maybe, tomorrow, I could go and see if there was another note. PLEASE COME IN MY GARDEN, TARA. Maybe.

The next morning I woke with a start. Nan was still asleep. I couldn't remember what was wrong at first, then my dreams cleared away, and I knew. But I had to get up and make sure.

There was no note. Nothing had changed, but the tools were still there, waiting. Surely Mr Barenstein should have taken them away? I looked round, as if there might be a clue somewhere. There was nothing. No footprints on the wet grass, no note.

But something was different. What? What had changed? Something had happened.

It was the pear tree. A house had appeared in it, like a house in a story. A tree-house. There were wooden walls and a roof. There was a rope ladder hanging down.

'A tree-house!' I whispered. I walked across the garden as if the pear tree was reaching out its arms and pulling me in to them. I touched the ladder with my finger, and the rope swung. I smelled the new wood. I wanted to climb that ladder more than anything on earth.

'Tara!' came a voice behind me. It was Mr Barenstein. He was there, outside, in the garden, for the very first time. He looked pale and papery and old, but he was smiling at me.

'I'm just looking at it,' I said quickly.

'It's all right, little girl. Go on.' Mr Barenstein nodded towards the tree-house. 'Go on.'

I grasped the rope. Step by step I swung myself up into the tree-house. My hands seemed to know their own way, and when I touched the branches of the pear tree they felt just as I had always imagined they would. And then I was high up, part of the tree, looking down at Mr Barenstein.

'Has he done a good job?' asked Mr Barenstein.

'What? Who?'

'Mr Giovanni. He built that house for me yesterday. Has he done a good job?'

I looked around the tree-house. I still didn't understand what Mr Barenstein meant. How could Mr Giovanni have made this, when he never came into the garden? The floor was made of planks, and the walls were made of planks and board. They were smooth when I touched them. Sunlight squeezed through chinks in the walls and danced on the floor. There was a door frame, and a window frame. It was a perfect little house, high in the tree.

'It's beautiful,' I said. 'It's beautiful.' But I wondered how Mr Barenstein was going to climb the ladder to get up into his tree-house. I'd never heard of a grown-up having a tree-house, but then Mr Barenstein was not like anyone else I knew.

'Shall I come down so you can come up?' I called. Mr Barenstein shrugged and shook his head.

'No, no,' he said. 'The tree-house is for the garden, not for an old man. And for anyone who likes the garden. Maybe you know someone who likes the garden? Someone who works hard to make the garden beautiful?'

And he smiled up at me, as if there was a joke shared between us. But I couldn't believe it yet. It was too much, and too strange. Did he mean me? Was the tree-house for me to go in? Was he really pleased with my work, after all? He was smiling at me. I couldn't disbelieve his smile. Yes, he really wanted me to be in the garden. I climbed down the ladder, and faced Mr Barenstein.

'Thank you,' I said. He made a little movement with his hand, as if he didn't want me to say any more. He was staring at me, and his face was sad.

'I had a sister once,' he said. 'She was younger than me. Unless my memory is playing tricks, she looked very much like you. And in our garden, when I was a child, we had a pear tree like this one.' He paused, and stroked the rough black bark of the tree.

'And one day,' he went on, 'my sister Hannah climbed into the tree. She was about your age, Tara. She climbed right up into the highest branches and she started to pull off the blossom. Just like that, in big handfuls, all white. She threw the blossom down over our mother, as if our mother was a bride.'

'What did your mother do?' I asked.

'Well, she laughed. It was a funny thing. But she was a little bit cross too, and she said to my sister Hannah, "If you pick the blossom, we shall have no pears." '

'What did Hannah do then?'

'Hannah looked at our mother and she laughed some more, and she tore down more blossom. More and more white blossom falling over everything.'

I didn't want to ask any more questions. I didn't want to know about his mother's anger, and Hannah's punishment. I wanted to think about Hannah laughing high up in the tree.

'My mother could not be angry,' said Mr Barenstein. 'She wanted to be angry, she tried to frown and scold. But when Hannah laughed you could not help laughing with her. Yes, she was your age,' said Mr Barenstein again, looking at me as if he saw someone else. 'When I saw you there in the garden, I almost thought I was seeing my sister Hannah again.' He leaned on his stick.

It was strange to think of Mr Barenstein having a sister who was young enough to climb to the top of a pear tree. I'd never known that he had any family. Nobody came to visit him. Probably Hannah was old now, much too old to climb into a tree.

'Mr Barenstein,' I asked, 'where is your sister now? Where is Hannah?'

For a long time Mr Barenstein did not answer. Then he said, 'That was a long time ago, Tara. Hannah died in a war, many years ago. They did not only tear down the fruit, they tore down the blossom, too.'

I said nothing. I didn't really understand what he was saying, but I understood that it was something old and terrible, that could not be changed. Then Mr Barenstein smiled his old, creaky smile.

'Go up in the tree-house again, Tara,' he said. 'I think you are good at climbing. As good as my sister Hannah!' And he waved his stick to say goodbye, and walked slowly away.

I sat in the tree-house, high up, and looked down at the garden. Soon I would go in and tell Nan all about the tree-house, but not yet. It was the most beautiful tree-house in the world. It was like a real house. Maybe I could even sleep up here, one night. But just for now I wanted to sit still and feel the pear tree gently rocking in the breeze, and look down on the fresh brown earth and the big pile of weeds, and think about Hannah.

The Airman's Sixpence

She keeps me up with her every night. It's as if she doesn't want to be alone. Even though it's nearly eleven o'clock now, she's just put three more big logs on to the fire. My cocoa steams on the wonky tin tray. She keeps back enough milk for my cocoa every night, and even sugar. Two spoonfuls. She always saves her sugar ration for me. There are biscuits as well. She watches me eating and her face is hungry. It's no good trying to hide a biscuit for Billy. She sees every move I make.

'Drink up, dear. Don't you like your cocoa?'

'Mmm, yeah. Course I do,' and I pick up the thick white mug.

'There's no need to say "yeah", Ruby. After all we aren't Americans.'

'No, Mrs Penbury.'

'Auntie Pauline, dear! You silly girl.' And she laughs, a tinkly laugh that's a bit frightening because it doesn't seem to belong to her. Mrs Penbury is big and she's as strong as any man. She does a man's job. She's always telling us that. Men have to be hard.

The wind whines round the farmhouse. It sounds as if it's fingering the walls, trying to get in to us. But I don't mind the wind. I strain my ears for what I think I can hear under it. Yes, there it is. A sound that's even thinner, even sadder than the wind. I glance quickly at her, and clatter my mug down on the tray to cover the sound. Has she heard? She's frowning, staring at her feet. What if she gets up, goes to the stairs, listens? What if she hears him? I'm sure it's Billy. He'll have had another of his bad dreams.

Billy's five. He never used to have bad dreams, till we came here. We were in London before, with Mum, then before that we were down in Devon, with Mrs Sands. She was lovely. But she couldn't take us back when the bombing started again, because her daughter Elsie had a new baby. Mum didn't want to send us away again, but she got a job in the factory at nights, and that meant she couldn't take us to the air-raid shelter if a raid started. I would've taken Billy. I'm old enough. But Mum wouldn't let me.

'No, Rube. With you and Billy safe in the country, at least I've got peace of mind. I know I'm doing right by you.'

It was all right in Devon with Mrs Sands. We missed Mum, of course we did. But not like this. Not with a pain that gets worse every morning when I wake up and know we've got another day here.

It *is* Billy. I know it is. He's crying again. He isn't properly awake yet, or he wouldn't make a sound. He's crying in his sleep. I shuffle my feet, crunch my biscuit, slurp the rest of my cocoa.

'I'm ever so tired, Auntie Pauline. I think I'd better get to bed.'

She stares at me. 'I've only just put those logs on the fire,' she says. 'Don't you want to sit up a bit longer?'

She always wants me to sit up. I don't think she wants to be on her own. She likes me to keep talking, it doesn't matter what I say. When it's quiet she looks as if she's listening out for things I can't hear.

But I've got to get to Billy. I stand up, and put down my mug. I'm supposed to kiss her goodnight now. I've got to do it. She mustn't know that I don't like kissing her, or she'll be worse than ever to Billy. Her hair bristles against my face.

'G'night, Auntie Pauline.'

'Goodnight, Ruby. There's a good girl.'

There's a little oil lamp for me to carry up and undress by. Billy has to go up in the dark. She pretends it's because he's too young to remember about the blackout, and he might show a light. Billy is frightened of the dark.

I go up the creaky stairs with my lamp flame shivering and bobbing on the walls. They are rough, uneven walls, because this is an old house, right on the edge of the village and well away from the other houses. It's a lonely house. Maybe that's why she wants me to sit up with her, even though at home Mum would've sent me to bed ages ago. The whimpering sound is getting louder. I hurry. She mustn't hear it. I know what to do. I've got to wake him up really gently. I kneel down by his bed and put my arms softly round him. He's sitting up but I can tell he's still asleep. His eyes have that funny nightmare look in them. He is cold. I cuddle him close and whisper, 'Billy, it's all right. It's only me. It's Ruby.'

I keep on cuddling and whispering. Slowly his stiff body relaxes. I can feel him coming out of the dream and waking up. I press his face into my shoulder to hide the noise.

'It's OK, Billy, Ruby's here.'

He's shaking. Perhaps he's ill? But I look at his face by the oil lamp and I see he's crying. Fear pounces on me.

'Oh, Billy. You haven't. You haven't gone and done it again.'

And he nods his head, crying and shivering.

'Never mind. Don't cry. Ruby's here.' I hold him tight, tight. He's only five. My little brother, Billy.

'*You look after Billy, Rube. You know how he gets his asthma.*'

That's what Mum said when she was waving us off on the train, the second time we were evacuated. She thought it would be like Mrs Sands again, and so did we. Billy was all excited, jumping up to look out of the window, waving at Mum. '*You look after Billy.*' Yes, I was right. He's wet himself. It's not his fault. It happens when he's asleep. He can't help it. But she mustn't find out. What can I do?

I can't do anything. She'll find out. She always does. And she'll put Billy in the cupboard under the stairs again, for hours and hours. It's dark in there. She says it's to teach him. *'He can't go on like this, Ruby. What'll your mum say when she gets him back, wetting the bed every night? She'll think I don't know what's right. Sometimes you've got to be cruel to be kind.'* He doesn't cry or scream when he's in the cupboard. I think she thinks he doesn't care. Oh, Billy. *'He's a boy, Ruby. No good bringing him up soft. You won't be doing him any favours.'*

Suddenly I make up my mind.

'Stand still, Billy, while I get your clothes. We're going home.'

I scrabble through the drawers. Clean pants, clean trousers, Billy's warmest jersey. His winter coat is on the hook downstairs. I'll get him dressed then we'll both get into bed and wait, wait . . . Once she's gone to bed, we'll go. We'll go home. Mum wouldn't want us to stay here. I know she wouldn't. She'll be working now, she works nights in the factory, but by the time we get to London it'll be morning. I don't care about the bombs.

When the last sound of Auntie Pauline going to bed has died away, we wait to give her time to go to sleep. I've blown out the lamp and it's dark. But I know my way round the house, even in the dark. I know all its lonely corners.

'Billy. Ssh. Hold my hand.'

The stairs don't creak. The kitchen door opens and there's

the smell of the slack she's put on the fire to bank it up for the night. Billy presses up behind me while I slide the big bolt back, very very slowly. It squeaks like a mouse. She hates mice. She's always leaving poison for them. The yard door swings open and black cold night air fills the space in the door frame.

'Wait there, Billy. Don't move.'

I sweep my hand along the dresser. There it is. Her fat black purse with the big clasp. I weigh the heavy purse in my hand. My mum always said she could leave a penny out on the kitchen table all week.

'Ruby'd never touch it. Would you, Rube?'

'No, Mum!'

I was so proud of that. Mum let me go to her purse and get the shopping money out, because she knew I'd never take a penny off her. Now I unsnap Auntie Pauline's big purse and feel inside. Two heavy half-crowns. A couple of joeys. A sixpence and a florin. I take them all and wrap my handkerchief round them. Is it enough to get us to London?

I hold Billy's hand tight as we shut the kitchen door behind us. The yard is full of shadows and we dodge through them to the gate. The lane is a tunnel of night.

'We can't go through the village,' I whisper to Billy. 'All the dogs'll bark at us. We'll go down the lane and across the fields.'

My chest hurts. Billy's too little, he can't run like I can.

I hoist him up, but he's too heavy for me and I can't carry him for long. He runs a bit, then I carry him, then he runs again. Each time I pick him up he's heavier.

'You're a good runner, Billy!' I tell him, to keep him going.

The wind rustles the trees over our head. There are sudden shapes and shadows. Something barks. Maybe a fox. We know about country things now. Then we come round the corner of the lane and a bit of moon shines on a big puddle. The road forks three ways.

'I got to put you down, Billy.'

He flops up against me. It's his asthma. Mum never *ever* lets him go out at night.

'All right, Billy, we'll have a rest.'

There's a stile and a path going across the fields. But no signposts. They've taken them all down in case the Germans come. Just the three lanes pointing off into the dark, and the path across the fields. Nowhere to say where the railway station is.

'You better now, Billy?'

He looks up and nods. I know he isn't really. I stare round, trying to guess, trying to remember which direction the station is. We came from the station, off the London train. But it all looks different in the dark, strange and different.

'You wait here a minute while I look down the lane.'

But he grips me tight. 'Don't leave me, Rube!'

That's when I see it. A little red light that grows strong in the dark under the trees, then fades. Then it brightens again. I know at once what it is. My mum smokes and sometimes she comes in and sits on my bed in the dark and I watch the red tip of her cigarette winking at me. Someone's smoking, there under the trees. Someone I can't see. I grab hold of Billy. As we stare, a big shadow peels away from the trees and moves into the lane. It's a man. A man smoking. A man in uniform.

I know all the uniforms. I peer through the dark and I see the shape of him. RAF. Straight away I feel a bit better. I like the RAF. He'll be on his way back to camp. Probably been to a dance. He throws away the cigarette and it skitters down the air and dies on the wet road. Then he walks slowly towards us as if he's been waiting for us, as if he knew we were going to come.

'Hello.'

I don't answer. But Billy pipes back, 'Hello' to him.

'You're out late,' says the airman. He's got a village voice, not a London voice like us. He must be from round here. I wonder where?

'Yeah,' I say. I look at him hard. Is it OK to ask him? I can see him quite well now because the clouds have blown back from the moon. But there's the shadow of his cap, too, hiding him. I clench my hand in my pocket, and it knocks against the money I've stolen.

She'll be after me. She'll get me. They'll all believe her. *A thief. A little thief.* No one'll believe I had to do it because of Billy, except Mum. I've got to get to Mum.

'We've got to catch a train,' I say. 'My mum's ill.'

'Oh,' he says, 'the London train? The milk train?'

'Yeah. The milk train.'

Then I think, *How did he know it was London I wanted*? But I don't ask.

'It's this way,' he says, pointing across the fields. 'It's only a mile, across the fields.' Then he says, 'I'll go with you. Make sure you get there safe.'

Everything my mum's told me about strangers floods into my head.

'It's all right,' I say quickly, 'we can find it.'

'Over this field. Turn left at the stile and follow the hedge. Then there's a gate. Straight over and across that field and you come to the road. Turn right and it takes you all the way.'

'Is there a bull?' asks Billy in his growly voice. He thinks every field's got a bull in it.

'Couple of cows if you're lucky. Turn left, keep going, cross the gate, keep going, turn right at the road. You got that?'

'Yeah.'

'Mind you look after Billy.'

Did he say that or was it my mum's voice in my head? No, he did. How did he know Billy's name?

'You got money for the train?'

My hand closes over *her* hard, cold coins.

'I got money.'

He looks at me. 'You took it, didn't you? You don't want to go taking her money.' He digs his hand in his pocket and brings out a handful of notes and coins. He picks out two pound notes and a ten-shilling note and holds them out to me. But I step back.

'It's all right,' he says. 'You take it. I've no use for it now.'

So I do. I feel as if I've got to do what he says. Then he gives Billy a sixpence. 'Buy some sweets with it,' he says. Billy looks down at the sixpence and up at the airman. He doesn't smile or say thank you. Billy's always quiet when he's pleased. The man puts his hand on Billy's head, and rumples his hair as if he knows him.

'Give me that money of hers,' he says to me, 'I'll put it back for you. Then you're all straight.' I like the way he says it, as if he knows how I'm always all straight at home, with Mum. I'm not really a thief. I give him the handkerchief, and he unknots it and takes out the money. He puts it away carefully, in a separate pocket from his own money, then he looks at us again. This time the moon is full on his face. He is sort of smiling, but not quite, and under it he looks sad.

He reminds me of someone. He looks like someone.

'Don't hold it against her,' he says. 'She can't help herself.'

I say nothing. He sounds as if he knows Auntie Pauline better than I ever could.

'Go on, then,' he says. I climb the stile, then he swings Billy up and over. I take Billy's hands and jump him down. 'I'll stand here,' says the airman. 'Just to make sure you take the right turning.'

When we get to the other side of the field we look back and he's still there. He waves, pointing left, and I wave back to show I know what he means. Then we climb up the next stile, and over, and the hedge hides him. We go as fast as we can. There's no time to talk, but once we're safely on the road, Billy pants out in his growly whisper, 'He's still watching us.'

'How d'you know?'

'He just is.'

The wind blows round us, cold and sweet and smelling of cows and country things. We stop to catch our breath and listen. Ahead of us there's the shunting noise of a train and I know we're nearly there.

'Don't worry, you're not going back,' says Mum. She's been working all night. She's worn out and here we are on the doorstep and what's she going to do with us? But it doesn't matter. Nothing matters now we're home. Billy's thinner and his chest sounds worse and when I tell Mum about the cupboard under the stairs she says she's going straight down the evacuation office to sort it out this very minute and we're not to move till she gets back. She goes off without even changing out of her overalls.

It's a long time before Mum comes back. Billy's asleep and I think I've been asleep too. Things are all muddled up in my head. The airman, the dark lane, the feel of Auntie Pauline's money. How could he put it back? Mum flops into her chair and shuts her eyes.

'They're going to get on to her,' she says at last. 'Course there's always another side to the story. Did she ever talk to you about her son, Ruby?'

'I didn't know she had a son. She didn't like boys.'

'He was in the air force. Died on a bombing raid last year. That's why she took you kids in, for the company. It must have been hard for her. Sent her a bit peculiar, I daresay, all on her own out there in the middle of nowhere, grieving for him. Not that it's any excuse, mind.'

'Don't be too hard on her. She can't help herself. Give me the money, I'll put it back.'

Mum sighs. 'I could murder a cup of tea,' she says.

'I'll make it,' I say quickly. I want something to do.

'Good girl. Seems she was so proud of him, being in the RAF. Oh, this war's got a lot to answer for. I suppose it got to her, other people's kids being all right when hers had gone.'

'But she was all right to me.'

'You're a girl, Rube. You wouldn't've reminded her of her son.'

I remember what Auntie Pauline was always saying, '*No good bringing a boy up soft. You're not doing him any favours.*' Was she thinking of her boy, and the war that was waiting for him when he grew up? I put the match to the gas and wait for the kettle to boil. I listen to the water begin to hiss in the bottom of the kettle. It's a sleepy, peaceful sound, and I shut my eyes.

Moonlight shines on the airman's face. He looks like someone I know. Who is it? The answer itches at the back of my mind but I can't quite reach it. He smiles. Then I know. It's Billy. The airman looks like Billy. So that was it. Mum was right, it was because Billy reminded Auntie Pauline of her own son that she was so hard on him. But perhaps she didn't mean to be. Perhaps she thought she was doing the right thing . . .

The kettle changes its note and starts to sing. I open my eyes and look at Billy, sleeping on the kitchen settle. His face has a bit of colour in it again. His hand is shut tight, even though he's asleep, and in it there's the airman's sixpence.

The Old Team

My brother Adam sits by the window, staring out, staring at nothing.

'I've got some calls to make in Nether Sowden. Why don't you come along, Adam? I'd be glad of the company,' says Dad, in the deliberately cheerful voice he uses all the time with Adam now. Adam turns away from the window and frowns, looking at Dad. His hands are curled into fists.

'Can't you leave me alone?'

'I was only asking –'

'I know. I know you were only asking. *But I don't want to come.*'

He gets up and walks heavily out of the room. We hear his feet clumping upstairs, back to the attic where he spends most of his time now.

'What does he do up there all day?' Dad asks me.

'He reads,' I say, though I know Adam doesn't read. He sits in a fog of silence, and I can't find a way through it.

'Brooding,' says Dad. 'That won't do him any good. He ought to get out and about. It'd take him out of himself.'

Dad rubs his face hard with the backs of his hands, as if he's trying to rub something away. 'You can't expect him to be just as he was,' he goes on. 'It'll take time. Don't say anything to your mother.' He goes out of the room too, and I hear the creak of the stairs. Is he going up after Adam? I wish he would. Dad's a doctor, he ought to be able to help somehow. Then he stops. After a while his footsteps come down, go across the hall, and out to the garden.

You can't expect him to be just as he was. I know that. I know how lucky we are that he's here at all. I've got my brother here at home, not like Danny Forrester, or Tony Loblow. Sometimes I think about what would have happened if Adam hadn't been wounded in March. A Blighty one, that's what it's called: a wound that was serious enough to get him sent home, but not bad enough to kill him.

The Germans started their big advance on 21st March. If Adam hadn't been wounded, he'd have been in the worst of the fighting. Half the battalion was killed, he told me. Doesn't Dad know that? Bannerman's dead. Bannerman used to get more parcels from home than anyone. He used to get roast chicken and fruitcake and wine and tinned oysters. He always shared them out. 'Dig in before the rats get it,' he said. Adam told me that. He told me about Oliver, who kept a pet mouse which ate everything except cheese. I wonder if the mouse escaped, or if he's dead too? Adam's best friend in the company was Carter. Carter was going to come and stay with us on his next home leave. He was going to teach me to play the mouth organ.

Adam talks to me, a bit. He told me about Carter being killed by a shell, then he said, 'I should have been with them.'

'But you were wounded, Adam,' I said. 'You couldn't have fought like that.'

Adam wouldn't listen. 'I should have been there,' he repeated. 'You don't know what it's like, Bart. If I hadn't got this shrapnel in my shoulder –'

'If you hadn't got shrapnel in your shoulder you'd be dead, too,' I said. I was angry. It sounded as if he didn't want to come back to us. As if he didn't even want to be alive.

Two years ago Adam was on home leave before he went out to the front in France. So many men had gone from our village already. On Sundays the church had a lopsided look, full of women and children. Adam told me how Mrs Quignall had asked him to take a message to Sam, even though Adam was in a different battalion and wouldn't be in the same sector of the front. She'd got a medal for Sam to wear round his neck. It was supposed to have the power to stop a bullet. Adam weighed the medal in his hand.

'Will you take it?' I asked.

'Course I will,' Adam said. 'You never know, I might meet up with some of the old team out there.' He meant the cricket team, the team he'd played for every summer since he was fourteen. He smiled, and said, 'What do you bet old Georgie's bowling fast ones to those Jerries, Bart?'

I smiled, but I was frightened. I didn't want Adam to go to France, even though I knew he had to. There wasn't any other way. The war had already been going on for two years. At the beginning everyone thought it would be over in a few months, but now it seemed as if it could go on for ever. There didn't seem to be any reason for it to stop. There would be more and more littl'uns wearing black armbands, more and more women dressed in black, and fewer and fewer men.

Adam's wound is healing. He was wounded in the right shoulder, but he's left-handed. He could still play cricket if he wanted to. But whenever I ask if he'll come out and bowl for me, he just says, 'Where's the use? The team's all gone.' *Jem Forrester, Mikey Loblow, Sam Quignall, Jackie and Budge Linklater, Georgie Low, Tom Low, Paul Quick.* And all the others.

Georgie Low got hit by shrapnel too, but much worse than Adam. His wound went gangrenous and he had to have his leg cut off. He sits in a cane chair in the kitchen all day long. He can still feel his leg, even though it's not there. His father came up to our house to talk to my father. You could hear old Low all over the house. He's the blacksmith, and you have to yell out to make yourself heard in the forge. Georgie Low was going to be a blacksmith, too, but you can't be a blacksmith with one leg.

'He still feels his leg, see, Doctor, like it's as real as yours or mine. He cries out at night when it pains him. Can't you give him something for it?'

Then Dad talked to old Low for a long time, but I couldn't hear what he was saying. I went out into the garden, chalked a wicket on the stable wall, and practised my bowling. My action was getting a lot better. After a while Dad came out and walked up and down the lawn, his head bent. I wished he'd come over and watch me, but he didn't. I thought he was going to walk straight past me, but then he stopped, put his hand on my shoulder and said, 'Thank God you're only thirteen, Bart.'

I'm only thirteen. I won't be going to the war, not unless it goes on for twenty years like some people say it will. It's July 1918, and the war has lasted for four years already. Now it's summer again, bright and hot like the summer the war began. That was the year our team won the Sowden Downs Villages Cup. A man came and took a photograph of the team, most of them standing, some sitting cross-legged on the grass. Timmy Ripley reckoned he'd got a wasp in his trousers and it took the photographer half an hour to get enough order to take the picture. Timmy's still out in France. His ma had a field postcard from him last week.

There they all are in the photograph, Adam in the middle holding the Cup, Georgie Low frowning because the sun was in his eyes, standing there with his arms folded. Georgie Low was our best fast bowler. He used to come up to the house every day in the summer holidays, when Adam was home from school, and they'd practise on the pitch we'd made in the old orchard.

'Can't we cut down some of the trees, Dad?' Adam had begged. 'Those apples are all maggots anyway. The trees'll make good firewood.' And in the end Dad had agreed. A couple of men came up from the village, chopped down the trees and grubbed up the stumps.

Once the long grass was scythed, we had a decent pitch. I was only six then, and so Adam must have been going on fifteen. I got sent to bed at seven o'clock, and I used to hang out of the window in the long light evenings, listening to the ball cracking against the bat, and the shouts of Jem Forrester, Mikey Loblow, Sam Quignall, Jackie and Budge Linklater, the Low boys. I couldn't wait till I was big enough to join in. Sometimes they used to let me field, and when no one else was there Adam would put me in front of the stumps, and bowl to me. He was teaching me to bowl as well, and when he was away at school I'd practise for hours against the stable wall, because that was what Adam had told me to do.

'You'll never be any good if you don't practise, Bart.'

I practised all right. Hour after hour, on my own but never lonely, thinking about what Adam would say when he came home on holiday and saw how hard I'd worked to improve. Sometimes I could almost hear him: 'You're coming on, Bart,' he'd say.

Jem Forrester's dead. Mikey Loblow's still out in France, like Timmy. Sam Quignall, Jackie and Budge Linklater, Tom Low, they're all dead. Sam was killed in training when a grenade went off in his hand. That's not what they said in the official letter, but Joe Farnell from Over Sowden was there and he saw what happened. He never told Mrs Low. Better for her to think he died fighting, but some of us know. Jackie and Budge are missing, believed killed. Tom died of wounds in April this year.

So there isn't any cricket team any more. There's plenty of littl'uns in the village who've never seen a decent game. The boys my age can remember what it was like when the village cricket field used to be mowed and rolled ready for Saturday. They only mowed a rectangle: the outfield was pasture, and you were lucky if there were sheep grazing on it, not cattle. Adam used to tell me about finding the ball deep in a cowpat when he was fielding. It's all long grass now, rough and tangled. You can't imagine playing cricket on it.

The visiting teams came from Over Sowden and Nether Sowden and all around. There was tea in the Village Hall – bread and jam and fruit loaf and iced fancies – and then afterwards there was beer in the *Crossed Hands* all night. The visitors would go wobbling off on their bikes, and then our team walked home in the dark, singing and swaying. Most times I'd be sent off home long before the night was over, but I remember once they let me stay, squeezed in between Jackie and Budge. Everywhere there were red faces roaring out songs and jokes I didn't really understand, but I laughed anyway, and I drank beer out of Budge's glass when he let me. All I wanted was to be with them. One day I'd *be* them, one of the team, sunburned and sweating, squinting my eyes against the sun.

It's July 1918. The team's gone, cricket's finished. That's what everyone in the village is saying, even when they don't open their mouths. There aren't any laughing faces in the *Crossed Hands* any more. Only old men. The black armbands say it's all over. Everything's over except the war, which will still be going on when everything else is dead. Adam's face says it too, when he sits staring at nothing. But I look down at my hand, grasping the cricket ball, feeling its smooth leather weight. I could drop the ball on the ground and walk away, but I don't want to. I want to bowl. I want to bat. I'm a fair batsman, a middling-to-good bowler, and not a bad fielder. A good all-rounder, that's what I want to be. I want to be better and faster. I want to learn everything I can. I need to learn now. It's not all over for me: it hasn't even begun. And I want my brother back.

I've got a plan. It's three summers since Dad last had the

pitch in the orchard scythed and rolled. The grass is long and tussocky, nearly as bad as the village cricket field. Hens get out of the henhouses and lay their eggs down there. You wouldn't believe that Adam and Georgie and the others used to play there. Dad didn't think it was worth bothering to keep the pitch, just for me. That's what he said, anyway. *When you're older, Bart. With the war, I can't get the men to do the work.* But I knew there was another reason. He didn't want to hear the sound of the ball clocking against the bat, or voices shouting in the orchard. Not while Adam was in France, in danger of dying every day. Not while telegrams were coming for the Lows, the Quignalls and the Linklaters. He wanted the grass to grow long and cover up everything.

But I'm not going to let him. It's no use asking him, so I'm going to do it myself. I'm not the only one. Danny Forrester'd play, so would Tony Loblow, and maybe Jake Martin, and there's others, littl'uns as well as the boys my age. We ought to be learning. *It's our turn.*

Tiny Metcham says he'll come up and scythe, after he finishes his work. He wants a shilling for it. He's six foot in his stockinged feet, and he says he's still the strongest man in the village, even though he's fifty-seven.

I asked Arthur Loblow about the roller (he's Mikey and Tony's grandad). 'It'll want greasing,' he says. 'You'll never move it. It takes a strong man.' Tony answered that me and him and Danny add up to a strong man, and then his grandad said if we thought we could do it, then good luck to us. He wasn't going to stand in our way.

Tiny Metcham found a nest with six eggs in it. Hen's eggs, speckled brown. He lifted the eggs up carefully and put them in his cap.

'You give these to your ma,' he said. 'Daft creature, laying away. Well, not so daft mebbe. It's nature to want to rear your own young 'uns, and keep a hold on 'em.'

I watch the scything, and I carry away armfuls of the fallen grass and spread them out to dry. It's quiet in the orchard, away from the house, hidden by the hedges. There's only the hiss of the scythe through swathes of grass, and the rasp when Tiny sharpens its blade on the whetstone. The pitch starts to appear, pale and shorn, bumpy with molehills. I measure it out. All the time I keep looking towards the house in case anyone comes, but no one does. I pay Tiny his shilling, and he thanks me and asks after Adam.

''Spect we'll be seeing him down the *Crossed Hands* one of these nights. He'll have to be getting his cricket boots on.'

'Yes,' I say.

Getting the roller up to the orchard is the worst job. Even with the three of us wrestling, it's a brute to move. First of all we spend hours sandpapering the rust off the rollers, and oiling it. It makes you want to kick it, it's so huge and heavy and filthy. It's been lying in a shed for three years. Tony and Danny and I swear as we shove and shoulder it out on to the lane. We're out of breath and sweating already. But we said we'd do it, and we're *going* to do it. I don't care who sees us now. If my dad does, I'd tell him what we're doing. Nothing's going to stop us.

We drag the roller up on to the newly-shorn pitch. My back hurts and there's sweat and streaks of black on our faces. Jake Martin saw us, and came to join in. He reckons his dad has a set of pads put away we could use. I don't want to ask Dad, or Adam: not yet.

Back and forth we stumble, all of us shoving at the roller handle, over molehills and ruts and tussocks, flattening them down. As we make a turn I think I catch a glimpse of something moving behind the hedge. I squint against the sun, which is sinking towards evening, but whoever it was, they've gone. As long as they don't stop us. Not now.

It's nearly dark when Tony says, 'Won't get it much more level than this.'

And we won't. It's not perfect, but it never was. It's good enough. Jake positions himself where the crease might be, and swipes with an imaginary bat.

'Coming up tomorrow, then?' I ask, and they all nod.

'We going to let the littl'uns come up?' asks Danny.

'We're going to need them,' I say. 'If we're ever going to get a team.'

It's hard to sleep. Adam's going to know tomorrow. As soon

as he hears the sound of the bat on the ball, and the voices, he'll know something's going on. And then what? I've planned it so far, but what's going to happen now? My mind races, while the smell of cut grass drifts in through my wide-open window. I wonder if Adam can smell it too.

After breakfast I go straight down to the orchard. Danny and Jake and Tony are there already, and they've brought a couple of littl'uns with them – the Harborne twins.

'You want to bat, Bart?' offers Jake.

'No, we'll put Tony in first, you, Danny, then me. Either of you littl'uns want to try? All right, Bertie next, then Al in last.'

I want to see what they can do. Same with the bowling. This is the start of building up the team. Al Harborne goes behind the wicket ('He's little, but he's tough,' says Tony), with Jake at long stop. Tony batting, Danny to bowl. I'm in the outfield, along with Bertie. The grass is almost up to Bertie's waist, but he's sharp-eyed and he swoops down on the ball when it rolls behind a patch of thistles.

Danny's not a bad bowler; at least he's accurate. Tony's strong, and he places his bat squarely to the ball. He hits a few singles off Danny's bowling, then we change over. They're warming up, getting going. Bertie throws well, and then he muffs an easy catch and his twin jeers. Bertie's face darkens. He makes for Al, but I haul him back. All the Harbornes are famous for fighting.

'You want to be in this team or not? And belt up, Al. This is a *practice*.'

I don't think about anything but the next ball. I don't notice the sound of the bat on the ball, or our shouts, or the way the noise carries. I don't hear footsteps, or see a shape moving behind the hedge. I don't see anything, and then I look up and there he is. My brother Adam, inside the orchard hedge, watching us. He stands there with his arms folded, like Georgie Low in that old photograph.

Tony's bowling now, to Jake. Tony runs up. Good action, nice ball. But Jake's seen Adam. His concentration vanishes, he fumbles trying to play a defensive shot, and he's clean-bowled.

I wave to Adam. He lifts his hand in a salute.

'I heard you,' he says. 'Thought I'd come down. Good game?'

'It's just a practice,' I say.

'You've got the old pitch in good shape,' says Adam.

'It's still pretty rough. It hasn't been used since –'

'I know,' says Adam. 'Carry on. Don't let me stop you.'

I hesitate. 'Do you want to –'

'I'll just watch,' says Adam.

This time Danny's batting. He's the best so far. He swipes the ball into the stinging nettles and gets two runs off it. Things are starting to take shape. Danny's back at the wicket. Then I look at Adam and for a second I forget everything. I don't watch the ball, or Danny, or any of them. I see what Adam sees. I see a different sun shining, casting different shadows. I see Jem Forrester running up, and then Jackie Linklater leaping for the catch off Sam's bat. I hear the clock of the ball, and Jackie's yell. Sun streams in their faces, and their shirts stick to their backs with sweat. This is *their* place, and it always will be.

Then they vanish, and there's only Adam, staring across at me.

'What are you playing at? You missed that catch,' he says.

'I was –'

'You were woolgathering,' he says. 'You can't do that. Not when you're playing cricket.'

'So were you,' I say.

The practice has stopped. The others are looking at us, curious and uneasy.

'Get back to it,' says Adam. 'You were doing fine.'

'How long've you been watching?'

'Long enough.'

'You reckon you could come down and coach us some time?'

We're all looking at him now, hoping. At last, slowly, he says, 'I'm not doing the work for you. It's *your* team. But I'll coach if you like, when I can. I'm not going to be here long, Bart. You know that.'

And I find I do. Adam's got to have a different life, and it can't be here, where there are ghosts for him on every patch of ground.

'All right,' I say. 'Tomorrow?'

'Tomorrow.' Adam nods, and turns to walk up to the orchard gate.

As I watch him go, I see them again. Budge and Jackie, Mikey and Jem, Paul Quick, Sam Quignall. They close in around my brother. They walk away together, arms round one another's shoulders, the light of the evening sun catching the backs of their heads. And then they are gone, and I know I'll never see them again.

I turn back to my team.

The Mars Ark

We weren't allowed to play out any more. In the evenings our back lane and pavements were empty. No bikes. No skateboards. No voices. No kids ringing our bell and asking, 'Can you come out?' It had been getting worse for a long time. There just wasn't enough air. At first you only felt it when you ran too fast, or biked too far. Then people started collapsing in the streets. If they were lucky someone would see them from a house and rush out with an oxygen mask. It happened to me once. I'd been climbing trees, and when I came down I felt dizzy and I couldn't see properly. Then Dad was bending over me and I heard the hiss of the oxygen mixture as he held a mask over my face.

Then there was the sun. It burned through everything: sunblock, sunhat, loose cotton clothes, all the stuff we'd been told to wear. The sun flamed white in the sky like a bully which knew it was much stronger than us. It could knock us down any time it wanted. None of us went out unless we had to. Our houses had air pump systems, and oxygen seals round doors and windows. Then the schools closed. No school, no playing out, no visiting friends.

Project Rescue One took away half the kids on our street. My best friend Nick went with it. Plane load after plane load of kids was airlifted to Siberia, with a few grown-ups to look after them. There were still green fields in Siberia, and streams, and crops growing. They told Nick he'd be able to play out there. Go fishing. Even swim. It was hard to believe. I asked Mum and she looked away and said, 'Well, it's better than staying here. But it won't last that long. It's not the answer.'

Mum knows. She's a climate scientist. Mum couldn't leave her job, so we stayed in our house, breathing the purified, oxygenated air that came through the wall-vents. Sometimes I wondered how long it would keep coming. Me, and Mum and Dad. And Bridget. Bridget was my hamster, and I'd had her for nearly a year. She was fudge-coloured with a white patch on her back. She used up oxygen, but not very much. Some kids I knew weren't allowed to have pets any more. My friend Alex had a dog, but it had to be put down. His mum didn't want to do it, but there was no choice. Their air allowance was for two adults and two children only, and the air officials said a dog took as much air as a human being.

Mum and Dad didn't write Bridget down on our air allowance form. I'd hidden her in an old trainer box inside my wardrobe, just in case. Later on I got her out and held her. She sat up and cleaned her paws and her whiskers and looked at me as if she knew exactly what was going on.

I'd always wanted to breed from Bridget, but I'd given up hope. People kept their pets secret now. Then one day a boy who used to be at my school rang me up. Luke was mad about animals. He'd had a snake in a tank, four gerbils, a white mouse, a couple of hamsters and a pet toad which he kept in the garden. As I picked up the phone I wondered how many pets he had left now. Luke came straight to the point.

'Joe. You still got Bridget?' Trust Luke to remember Bridget's name. Animals were like people to him. And he was too clever to say the word 'hamster' on the phone. You never knew who might be listening.

'Yeah,' I said, 'Bridget's fine.'

'How old is she?'

'Only about a year. Ham – I mean, they can live much longer than that, can't they?'

'Only about another year. That's why I phoned you. Listen. D'you remember Glory? Male, one year old, chocolate brown. You don't often get them that colour.'

'Oh, yes –' Luke had brought his hamsters into school one day. I remembered a dark one.

'I think Glory should meet Bridget,' said Luke. 'The way things are now, we don't know how many of them are left. They don't live very long. We've got to do something!'

Luke was right. There might be just a handful of single hamsters, hidden by their owners. And I'd always wanted Bridget to have babies. Chocolate coloured babies . . . mole-coloured babies . . . fudge-coloured babies . . . 'Yes,' I said to Luke, 'we've got to do it.'

How were we going to get Bridget and Glory together? You couldn't even walk down the garden any more. Then I thought of Mum and the car. She had special privileges because of her job. She was working on a computer projection about oxygen loss from the earth's atmosphere. Mum was always having to go on the Space Hopper to the Moonbase to collect data. And for local trips she had a permit to use her car, even though nearly all cars and buses and trains were banned.

'Mum! Please! Luke's house is only a few hundred metres off your route. I've looked at the map! Please, I've got to see Luke.'

In the end, they gave in. Mum would drop me at Luke's on her way to the research station, and pick me up when she came back. I didn't say a word about Bridget. I took my backpack with some computer games in it, and said I was going to swap them with Luke. And I took Bridget, safely hidden in the backpack, nestled up in her bedding with sunflower seeds to keep her happy. I hadn't been anywhere for so long that I was looking forward to seeing all the places I knew. But it was all scorched and empty. Dark brown lawns. Empty streets. Piles of leaves from trees which were nearly bare, though it was only June. Empty shops, and our school playground with no kids in it. The bully sun chased us all the way, bouncing off our car bonnet, dazzling in through the windows and hurting my eyes.

Luke's hamster came slowly and grumpily out of his bedding, half asleep.

'Give him a minute,' Luke said. 'He'll be all right.' I was worried in case Glory fought Bridget, but he didn't. After a few minutes nosing around, Glory got really excited. Perhaps Bridget and Glory were lonely too, even though hamsters like being alone most of the time. When they'd finished mating we separated them, and hid Bridget carefully back in her bedding.

'Just think!' said Luke. 'Bridget and Glory might be the very last pair of hamsters left in the world.'

'It'll be all right if Bridget has babies,' I said. 'Aren't all pet hamsters descended from one pair that was found in the desert?'

Luke's gerbils had gone, and the snake, and the white mouse, and his other hamster. The toad must have died. It couldn't survive in the brown, scratchy grass with nowhere to hide from the sun. Only Glory was left. And Bridget.

Mum looked tense as we drove home. Had she guessed about me bringing Bridget? I'd whistled quite loudly to cover up Bridget's scuffling.

'Mum,' I said cautiously, 'is everything OK?'

'It's all right, Joe. It's nothing you've done.'

Mum's hands were tight on the steering wheel, and she was pale, even though it was so hot. When we got home she asked me to go up to my room. She had things to discuss with Dad. I didn't mind, because I had to smuggle Bridget back into her cage. But the talking downstairs went on and on and on, and I began to get worried. At last I heard Dad call, 'Joe! Joe! Come down here a minute!'

They were sitting on the sofa and they made room for me to sit between them. Dad put his arm round me, and his face was pale too, like Mum's, so I knew it was something bad.

'Joe. You know your mum's job is very important?'

I nodded.

'Well, she's been chosen – selected – for a very special project.'

'Not Project Rescue One!' I burst out. I didn't want Mum going to live in Siberia.

'No, nothing like that,' said Mum. 'It's something you won't have heard about.'

'Something secret?'

Mum looked sad. 'Well, yes, I suppose so. The thing is, this new project can't take many people. It's very new – very experimental. It has to be monitored all the time, and that's why I've been chosen. It's called the Mars Ark.'

It sounded like a chocolate bar. What did Mum mean?

'You learned about the Mars Space Station at school, Joe, didn't you?'

'Yeah, of course we did. Ages ago.' We'd done it in year four and made models of it in art. Everyone did, just like you make models of dinosaurs. Some people said the Mars Station was about as much use as a dinosaur.

'There's a lot more to the Mars Station than they've ever made public,' said Mum. 'Since the big changes in climate began a few years ago, they've built a biosphere there: it's like a huge bubble where life can be kept going without help from outside. It's got its own air, water and soil. You can grow plants, trees . . .'

I tried to imagine a massive Kew Gardens whirling around Mars. Kew Gardens the way it used to be. It's all gone now. Thick fronds of fern, the sound of water, the smell of things growing. Birds darting from tree to tree. Green light and leaf shadows on your arms.

'It's ready for a few people to live there,' said Mum.

I gaped at her. 'Mum! You can't! You can't go off to Mars and leave us.'

'It's OK, Joe,' Dad broke in, 'we're all going. They need families now.'

I couldn't take it in. I'd been on the Space Hopper, like everyone else, and Matthew Spencer in our class had done the Moon Walk and boasted about it for weeks. But the

Mars Station! I could only think of my model getting dusty on our classroom shelf. I couldn't imagine going there. *Living* there.

'How long for?' I asked.

Mum didn't answer. She and Dad looked at each other, then I guessed.

'For ever?' I croaked.

They nodded. Their eyes were full of tears. Mum swallowed and said, 'We'll be monitoring the Mars Ark, but we'll also monitor the earth from there. We'll record all the climate changes.'

'Maybe it'll get better, one day,' said Dad, but even I could see he didn't think that would happen for a long time. And we'd be up there, in the Mars Ark. Families and children. Growing up. Spending all our lives there. Forgetting the earth we came from, and how beautiful it had been once. Then I had a thought.

'Mum,' I said, 'will we be able to play outside there? There'll be other kids, won't there?'

Mum's face cleared. I'd asked the right question. 'Of course, Joe. Of course there'll be other children. And you'll be able to play out any time you want. Except when you're in school.'

School! Oh. But in a way . . . I'd really missed it.

I wasn't allowed to tell anyone where we were going. I had to let them think it was Siberia. It was still hard saying goodbye, even on the telephone. No one saw us go. We set off just before dawn, in the hot, secret darkness. Transfer to Space Connect, transfer to Space Hopper, then the great grey Earthship swam into view, waiting for us, hanging there against the brilliant stars. I'll never forget how our blue and green world grew small outside my observation panel. It looked so perfect. It looked like the one place in that forest of stars where you'd want to live. I had my backpack with me, strapped down safely. Three computer games, my favourite books, photographs of our house, my friends, our school. And under it all, protected by a plastic box with holes in it, and padded with bedding and woodchips, there was Bridget. I was pretty sure they wouldn't let me take her, so I pretended I'd given her to Luke. The stars whirled and I shut my eyes. Beneath the noise of the Earthship I heard Bridget's small squeak.

On our first night in the Mars Ark I went to sleep to the sound of running water. A thick-leaved green plant grew by the door of our family bubble. The air was fresh. It smelled of things I hadn't realised I'd missed so badly: damp earth, water, leaves, animals. Our air on Earth hadn't smelled like that for years. I'd had to tell Mum and Dad about Bridget once we were there, but they weren't as angry as I thought they'd be. Mum stood by my bed to say goodnight, looking back in the direction of our Earth. Her lips moved and I knew she was remembering things. People.

I woke up at dawn. It was the Mars Ark dawn, carefully timed to imitate the real thing. Cool grey light filtered through the leaves, and I could hear them rustling, but that wasn't the sound which had woken me. It was something else, much closer. Tiny piping squeaks from Bridget's cage by my bed. My heart went tight in my chest. I thought Bridget must be ill, perhaps dying. The last hamster, and she was dying. I couldn't bear it. I didn't want to look, but I had to. And there she was, lying on her side in the cage we'd made for her the night before, in a nest of bedding she'd scrabbled together. And half-hidden under her, squirming and squeaking, were her babies. They hadn't got any fur yet so they didn't look much like hamsters at all, more like fat little pink worms. Their eyes weren't open yet. Seven baby hamsters. I counted them later, when Bridget left the nest for a few seconds to get a drink of water. They'd be chocolate-coloured and fudge-coloured and white-patched and mole-patched. Bridget's and Glory's babies. I wished Luke could see them. I remembered what he'd said, 'Just think! They might be the very last pair of hamsters left in the world.'

Well, they weren't now. Bridget snuggled round and one of the babies squeaked again. I couldn't wait to get to know the other kids so they could come and see the hamsters. I knew I mustn't disturb her now she'd had her babies, so I didn't try to stroke her. I looked at Bridget and she looked at me with her bright beady eyes. Then I whispered to her,

'Bridget, you're brilliant!'

And Bridget squeaked back.

Clyde's Leopard

I was with Dad when I first saw the leopard.

'There's something wrong with that creature,' Dad said. We stood in the rain and watched the leopard pacing up and down its cage, fast, its tail twitching. Its head was down and it wasn't looking at anything. Suddenly it banged against the bars as if it didn't know how big the cage was. The rain fell and it was getting dark, but I couldn't leave the leopard. It thudded into the side of the cage again, harder.

'Come on, Clyde. I don't know what you want to watch this for. Poor devil,' said Dad.

I didn't *want* to watch. I had to. All that power in its muscles. Its sleek skin tight over its shoulders. I heard the leopard's claws scrape on the concrete floor of the cage as it turned, and now its tail was lashing from side to side.

'I'm going to get one of the keepers. There's something not right,' Dad said. 'You wait here a minute, Clyde,' and he went off. I didn't move. All I wanted was for the leopard not to be here, for this not to be happening. The cage clanged as the leopard jarred against it again. It was going to start throwing itself against the bars. It was going to beat itself against those bars until it died.

But it didn't, of course. The keeper came running with Dad, and Dad made me go away. When we were in the car I said, 'What'll they do to it, Dad? They won't kill it, will they?'

'No,' Dad said, but he didn't sound too happy. 'They'll dope it. Give it a tranquilliser. Leopards are valuable animals.'

When I got home I went to my room and lay on the bed. I felt like the leopard, full of anger, wanting to hit against something. But there was nothing to hit against. I reached down and picked my sketchbook off the floor. I found a clean page and got my pack of drawing pencils. I started to draw the cage. Thick black lines going down, one after another. And bushes all round that were meant to make the cage look less like a prison. Inside, I drew the leopard, cut into stripes by the bars of the cage. I drew its head hanging down, and its shoulder muscles bunched with tension. Then I pushed the drawing away and looked at it.

It wasn't that good. It looked like any leopard in any cage. You couldn't see the anger. I flipped over to a clean page and began to draw again. This time the pencil knew what to do. I drew a tree, with thick twisted branches, and a canopy of leaves. And on one of the thickest, strongest branches, I drew the leopard. It lay along the branch, its body melting into the pattern of the tree. You'd have to look twice to see it. If you were down on the ground you'd never see it at all. The leopard lay as if it was part of the branch. Completely relaxed. But its head was up, watching, waiting. Any minute that long spotted body would pour off the branch and spring on to its prey. All around it, for miles and miles, there were trees and long, dry, golden grass. But I didn't draw all that, though I knew it was there. I just drew the leopard on its branch, waiting, watching. Ready to spring and run for miles if it wanted.

'Clyde!' shouted Mum from downstairs. 'CLYDE!' Her voice sounded as if she'd been calling me for a long time. I pushed the sketchbook under the bed and went down.

They'd been arguing again. The air was stiff with it. That was why Dad and I had gone to the zoo, because it was Sunday and if Mum and Dad did things together they always ended up arguing. I ate my pizza and looked down at the table and thought of the leopard, bounding over the long golden grass. I didn't hear anything they said.

That was last year, when I was still in Mr Davison's class. Things are different now. I don't do drawings any more.

I've been late a lot this term, but this morning I was really late. Registration was over, half the class were doing maths and the others were finishing their history reports. By the time Mrs Treece had stopped going on at me and I could slide into my chair it was quarter to ten. Matt looked up and said, 'Did you hear about the wall?'

'No, what wall?'

'The playground wall's going to be painted. There's an artist coming to do a mural.'

'Clyde! Please get your maths out and don't stop Matt working,' said Mrs Treece. She was in a really bad mood. She'd already said she was going to get Mum to come in and talk to her about me being late, so I stopped talking and scrabbled round for my books. But I couldn't think about maths. The ugly grey breeze block playground wall lay across my mind. I couldn't imagine that wall with a painting on it.

'He's coming this afternoon,' Matt whispered without looking at me.

'The artist?'

'Yeah.'

He came in an old white van with WASH ME written in the dirt on the back. He was the tallest man I'd ever seen. When Mrs Treece stood next to him her head only came up to his elbow. His eyes were very dark and shiny, looking down at us from high up.

'I'm Sam Florio,' he said. 'You can call me Sam.' He wore a black leather jacket without a speck of paint on it. He looked more like a biker than an artist. We were out in the playground, by the wall.

'OK,' he said, looking at us then at the wall. 'This is your wall so I want your ideas.' It was a sharp sunny day and the wall looked uglier than ever. Kids like Ellie Jones and Jonathan Gore jumped about with their hands waving wildly and ideas busting out of their mouths.

'We could have a rainforest background.'

'We could have all the animals that people are killing off.'

'Endangered species!' shouted Ellie Jones. I looked away, over the top of the wall. The mural wasn't going to be anything to do with me.

Sam Florio took off his leather jacket and laid it on the ground at the foot of the wall.

'But what do *you* want?' he asked. 'What do *you* like? Think about it.' Slowly, slowly, his eyes moved from face to face until he was looking straight at me. What did I want? I didn't want to think about it. Dad once told me, *Never let anyone know what you really want, or they'll make sure you don't get it.* Other kids' ideas went bouncing round the playground. Colours. Background. Big trees and birds like toucans and parrots. Colours flashing out against the green. There were too many ideas and I couldn't see how any of them could become real.

'But first of all,' said Sam Florio, 'we have to do the preparation. The boring bit, some people call it. I don't. This wall has to be scrubbed and primed or the paint won't last more than six months. It'll crack and come off. Anyone who wants to help, I'd appreciate it.'

I knew all about preparation. I used to help Dad in the holidays. Dad used the steam stripper to take off old wallpaper. I sanded and filled in holes. Sometimes the person whose house we were working in brought tea for Dad and juice for me. That was before Mum told Dad to go.

Not many kids wanted to help with the preparation. They moaned that they wanted to do *painting*, not clean up a dirty old wall. So Mrs Treece said I could work on the wall all afternoon if I wanted. I could see her thinking it'd be less trouble if I was out here. Matt and Martina Foster wanted to help as well. 'Four of us is plenty,' said Sam Florio. 'I'd rather have the ones who really want to do it than the whole class out here mucking about. They'll all get a turn with the painting later on.'

The wind was cold but the sun was bright and we soon got hot with working. I'd never seen anyone work faster than Sam Florio, not even Dad. Maybe it was being so tall. His hands were long and strong and sure. They scraped and scrubbed and primed like the hands of five men. The closer I got to the ugly old breeze block wall, the more I got to like it. I was beginning to see just how good it would look once it was painted. I liked the steady way we worked, with the sound of scrapers and the smell of priming paint all round us. If I shut my eyes I could almost believe that Dad was working beside me.

'Take a break,' said Sam Florio, as one of the kids from

class four came slowly across the playground carrying a wobbly tray with mugs of tea.

'Is that tea for us as well?' asked Matt.

'Sure. You've been working, the same as me.'

I spooned sugar into my mug of tea, the way Dad always did. You need sugar for energy when you're working. There was a packet of ginger biscuits, too. Sam Florio looked along the wall, inspecting the work, while we ate biscuits and drank tea.

'Soon have this finished,' he said. 'I'll work on till it gets dark, after you lot go home. Tomorrow it'll be dry.'

And then Ellie Jones and Jonathan Gore and the rest of them will be out here painting their ideas on to it, I thought. It won't be our wall any more.

'That question I asked you,' said Sam Florio. 'Have you got an answer yet?'

'What question?' asked Martina.

'What do you want on this wall?'

'An anaconda,' said Matt. It was true, I knew it. Matt loved snakes. He was saving up for a snake of his own, in a glass box in his bedroom.

'So, you'd like an anaconda on the wall?' asked Sam Florio. 'Sounds OK to me. It's a long time since I had the chance to draw an anaconda.'

Matt looked at me. It was a 'Go on, you say something now' look.

'Not a snake for you,' said Sam Florio, looking at me.

'No,' I said.

'Clyde can draw,' said Martina suddenly. 'He used to do brilliant drawings when we were in Mr Davison's class.'

I felt Sam Florio looking at me, but I wasn't going to look back. *Brilliant drawings*. I thought of the big green drawing book Dad bought me. 'Maybe you'll be an architect one day,' Dad said, 'they have to be good at drawing.' But I hadn't touched the book since last year. *Brilliant drawings*. It felt as if someone else had done them. When Mrs Treece gave out paints and paper, or drawing pencils, my hands just wouldn't work any more. But out here, in the sun, in front of the playground wall that was just waiting for paint, maybe, maybe . . .

'Tomorrow I start to draw the design on to the wall,' said Sam Florio. 'I'll be working on the design tonight, after I've finished here. See this notebook?' He tapped it. 'All your ideas are in here.' He snapped open the notebook and wrote in *Anaconda*. Then he put the notebook back down on the ground, in the pocket of his leather jacket.

'I'm going in for five minutes,' he said.

'Can we go to the toilet now?' asked Matt.

'Go ahead.'

Matt and Martina followed Sam Florio across the playground, but I stayed where I was. The door into school swung shut behind them. I was alone, with the high grey wall in front of me. Cleaning it and priming it had changed things. It wasn't just part of the school now. It belonged to me as well. I looked all round, then I bent down quickly and felt inside Sam Florio's leather jacket. There was the notebook. I flipped open the pages. They were covered in words and tiny drawings. A football boot kicking a ball, a girl running, the long branches of a tree brushing the ground. They must be drawings from other murals he'd done. They were good. I turned the pages until I found a clean one. There was a little pencil in the spine of the notebook. I took it out and looked round again. Then I crouched down with the book on my knee, took a deep breath, and drew.

It only took a few minutes. By the time Matt and Martina came out, the notebook was back in Sam Florio's jacket pocket.

The next morning I got in early, and went straight to the wall. Sam was there, drawing squares all over the wall.

'This is how I transfer the design,' he said. 'Each square on the wall matches a square on my design. It's all measured out. This way all the trees and animal should come out in the right places on the wall.'

'Can we see your design?' asked Ellie Jones, looking at the roll of paper that lay on the ground.

'Not yet,' said Sam. 'You'd better go on in now.'

It was time for registration, but I stayed there, watching.

Sam was numbering the squares. Then he stepped back to look at the wall, and saw that I was still there.

'Want to see the design?'

'I don't mind.'

He bent down and unrolled the paper. 'I've done a colour sketch too. This is the black and white, the one we use to help us get the drawing on to the wall.' The wind snatched at the paper as Sam smoothed it and spread it out. 'There.'

There was a background of thick trees, with twisted, muscly trunks and branches. There were toucans and parrots and an anaconda coiled up like a heap of rope. There were wild tangles of creeper and sploshes of flowers. It was good. Really good. The drawing was divided into tiny numbered squares, to match those on the wall. The left-hand part of the roll of paper had curled up again. Sam spread it out and held it down. 'Look,' he said. I looked, then looked again. On the thickest, most twisted branch there was a shape I knew. It lay there as if it had been poured on to the branch. Relaxed, as if it was sleeping. But it wasn't sleeping. The tip of its tail seemed to quiver with life. I could almost see it switch from side to side as it waited, waited . . .

My leopard.

'Nice piece of drawing,' said Sam.

'Yeah, it's good,' I said. He turned and looked straight at me. 'I meant yours,' he said. 'The leopard. All I've done is copy the drawing you did in my notebook, and scale it up.

See those squares on the wall? Three and four, eight and nine, thirteen and fourteen. That's where your leopard's going to go.'

I looked at the drawing, then at the wall. I could see just where the leopard would be, lying along the thick branch that twisted out of the canopy of trees. Hidden, until you looked twice.

'Here,' said Sam. He had a lump of chalk in his hand. 'Have a go. This wipes straight off if you don't like what you've done. See if you can scale up the drawing so it goes in the right place.'

He made it sound as if it was the easiest thing in the world. But my hand was clumsy as I took the chalk. Maybe I couldn't do it any more, not with him watching.

'It's your leopard,' said Sam. 'You know him better than anyone else.'

And suddenly I knew I could do it. He was my leopard. He was waiting, and the wall was waiting. I touched the chalk to the surface of the wall. It made a sudden mark, like a shout in silence.

'Go on. Look at the drawing, then go for it.'

And the chalk started to move. Once I began it was like swimming. You can't believe you ever thought you'd forget how to do it. The leopard grew under my hand. His long, rippling back, his huge cat-head. He lay along the branch as if he'd been born there. Any moment now he would spring off the branch. I stood back. He was there. The drawing had worked.

'That's fine,' said Sam.

All the breath I'd been holding went out in a sigh. It felt as if something was finished, even though I knew the real work had only just begun. The whole design had to be transferred on to the wall, and outlined in something that would last better than chalk if it rained. And then there'd be all the painting, with some kids being stupid and slopping paint around, and others only caring about their own bit, not about anyone else's. But I knew Sam wouldn't let them muck about with my leopard.

'It's a big job,' said Sam, 'but we've made a start.'

I was going to be late, really late. 'I've got to go in,' I said, and picked up my bag.

'See you later,' said Sam. I ran across the playground and pulled open the door. Then I looked back. Sam had started work again. Most of the wall was dull grey, ugly if you didn't know it close up. But I knew that wall now, every inch of it. And even from right across the playground I could see my leopard lying along its branch, ready to spring.

Wolf Weather

'There's the bus!' yells Mum. 'Quick, Jess! Run!'

I hear John Johnson the bus driver hit the horn as he comes over Hangshaw Fell. *Da da, da da da, DA DA DA*! The bus races down the hill towards the end of our track. He thinks he's going to beat me. *Da da, da da da, DA DA DA*! I really hate the way that horn sounds. I'll run my fastest and get to the end of the track before the bus.

But the mud's frozen. I trip and slide on deep tractor ruts. There's ice everywhere, thick white plates of it where there were puddles last night. All our sheep are huddled up against the wall, out of the wind. They look at me pathetically, as if they want me to help them, but I run on. I slip and slide and the wind pokes its freezing fingers through my jacket.

Snow, I think, snow, snow, snow.

Everyone says it's going to snow. Dad said it last night when he fetched the sheep in from the fell. Mum said it this morning when she made me find my boots and my scarf and my gloves. That's why I'm late. Snow. The first we've had this year. Maybe we'll get cut off. That'll be brilliant. No school bus, no horn blaring at me, no John Johnson.

'Run, Jess!' shouts Mum behind me. But I've got a hot sharp stitch in my side and the bus is going to win. John Johnson brakes at the end of our track. He leans out of the window and yells, 'Can you not get yourself up in the morning?' At least there are only Alice and Danny in the bus. We live farthest away from school and we get picked up first. By the time the bus gets near town there are twenty-five kids on it, and John Johnson makes them all shout at anyone who's late. *'Can you not get yourself up in the morning?'* And then there's his big red face grinning as you fall up the bus steps. I really hate John Johnson.

The bus is warm. I flop down beside Alice.

'You OK, Jess? D'you want some gum? Hey, guess what, Sinba's had five more kittens, but Mum says I can't keep any this time. Do you want one?'

'It's going to snow,' says Danny, leaning over the aisle, butting in as usual.

'We know that,' says Alice.

We're climbing, going up high to the top of the fell. There's ice on the road. I look down at the frozen fields and suddenly something Mum said this morning jumps into my mind.

'Wolf weather.'

'What d'you mean, Mum?'

'It's what my nan used to say. Wolf weather. When it's as cold as this, wolves used to come off the fell, down to the farms.'

'What, when your nan was little?'

'Don't be daft, Jess. Hundreds of years ago.'

We're nearly at the top when the bus engine starts to cough like my grandad. We slow down. The bus shakes all over and our seats rattle as the engine chokes. Alice grabs the front of the seat. The bus jerks and grinds and then suddenly the engine gives a long, whining wheeze. The bus slides a little way, then stops up by the drystone wall.

'The engine's gone,' says Danny.

'I know that, Danny Armstrong,' snaps Alice. John Johnson thumps the steering wheel with his fist and swears loudly. Alice and I look at each other.

'He's really horrible, isn't he?' whispers Alice. Then John Johnson opens his door and a knife of wind whistles in and moans round the bus like a ghost.

'Look!' says Danny. 'Snow!'

Big thick flakes pour out of the yellow sky, faster and faster, whirling in the wind. Now the sky is a white blur. It makes me dizzy to look at it.

'A blizzard,' says Danny.

'It's not a blizzard yet,' says Alice, but you can tell it's going to be one. Once it starts snowing like this it doesn't stop for hours. We'll be stuck. Already the road's covered with snow. We can hear John Johnson banging at the engine outside, but we can't even see him through the snow. I sneeze. Then John Johnson clambers back up the bus steps with snow all over his back, and snow in his hair. He glares at us as if the snow's our fault.

'There's no doing anything with it. I'll have to get to a phone and call for a breakdown truck. So you'll just have to stop here till I get back, and no fooling around. That means you, Danny Armstrong.'

'Blackcross Farm's nearest,' says Danny, 'you can go straight across the fields from here.'

'I know that,' says John Johnson, though I bet he doesn't.

'I'll show you the way if you like,' says Danny.

'You'll do no such thing. You'll stay here, and if you're not sitting there in that seat when I come back there'll be hell to pay.'

He fastens his jacket up tight and glares at us one last time before clumping down the steps. Alice and I stare through the window. He climbs the stone stile in the wall, and flounders off across the fields.

'Is he going the right way, Danny?' I ask.

'I hope he falls in a snowdrift,' says Danny, 'and stays there till next spring.' He feels in his pocket and brings out a white rustling bag. Sherbet lemons. He puts one in his mouth and sucks at it, looking at us. Danny never, ever shares his sweets. My mouth starts to tingle. It's a long time since breakfast. What if John Johnson doesn't find the farm? We could be here for hours. If it keeps on snowing like this it'll need the snowplough to get through to us.

It's getting colder and colder now the engine's stopped and the heater isn't working. The snow blows hard against the windows. I can't even see the wall any more. It's as dark as evening. The wind rocks and shoves against the windows.

'I'm going out to have a look,' said Danny.

'No, you're not,' says Alice. 'John Johnson said not to. You'll get lost and don't think Jess and me'll come looking for you.'

'Lost!' scoffs Danny. 'I know every inch round here.'

He does, too. But the wind moans and howls, 'Lost, lost, lost,' as if it knows something we don't know.

'They'll never find us,' I whisper.

'Don't be stupid,' says Alice, sounding cross. Alice always sounds cross when she's frightened. Then I hear something else, behind the wind. A thin, whining sound, far away. A whine, and then a howl. It's getting louder all the time. Coming closer.

'Someone's dogs are out,' I say. My voice sounds funny. We sit very still, straining our ears. It comes again, nearer now, a howl that rises up into the air and shivers like the sound of dogs baying to the moon.

'Those aren't dogs,' says Danny.

'They sound a bit strange,' says Alice, moving up a bit closer to me.

'They're coming this way,' I say. 'Listen!' The noise echoes round the bus. It's so close now that we can't tell where it's coming from. The howling winds round and round the bus, like the whirling of the snow. Danny doesn't say any more about going out for a look.

'Can we lock the door?' asks Alice.

Suddenly everything goes quiet. The wind dies and the snow falls straight and thick. The flakes stop beating against the bus windows, and we can see out a little way. Already the snow's curled in drifts by the walls and the road has gone. Everything's white. There is no sound at all.

'They've gone!' whispers Alice.

'Look!' says Danny, pointing. All the colour has emptied out of his face. 'Look!'

We peer out through the steamy windows, into the falling snow. *There's nothing but snow*, I tell myself fiercely. *Nothing but snow*.

Snow makes strange shapes as it whirls and falls. It makes you believe you can see anything. That dark shape, there. And that one, circling round. Those heads, those pricked ears. It's only the snow, making me see things. Another shape, and another. They are pouring over the wall like water. There are so many I can't count them.

'Jess!' Alice grabs my hand. 'What are they?' But she knows, and I know. *Wolf weather*, that's what Mum said. Snow and wind and cold. It drives them off the fells, down to the farms. The dark shapes lift their heads and howl and the sound they make is wilder and stranger and older than any sound I've ever heard.

'Wolves.' I don't know if it's me who says it, or Alice. The word makes the wolves real. Now they are so close I can see their long, narrow grey heads, their thin, hungry bodies. They are out hunting. They weave round and round the bus, making dark patterns on the snow.

'It's a pack,' says Danny, 'like a family.'

I look again and suddenly I see that he's right. There are young wolves and wolf cubs, running by their mothers' sides. There are old shaggy wolves and strong leaping wolves.

'They're looking for something,' whispers Alice.

'What?'

'Food,' says Danny, 'that's what they want. Food. Maybe they can smell us.'

'Wolves don't eat people,' I say quickly. I look from Alice to Danny. 'Do they?'

'Course they do. It's winter, Jess. They're hungry.'

'They can't get in the bus. The door's shut.'

Danny and Alice and I peer out through the snow at the circling wolves. There are even more of them now and they are close to the bus. If they leaped at the windows, would they break? If they threw their weight against the door, would it open?

'Alice. Have you got your sandwiches?' asks Danny.

'What d'you mean?'

'Your packed lunch. You've got sandwiches in it, haven't you?'

'Course I have.'

'Give them here. And you, Jess.'

'What are you going to do with them?'

'Feed them to the wolves.' Danny gives us a strange little grin.

'What, our packed lunches? They won't want them.'

'We've got to try. Quick!'

We scrabble in our bags and get our packed lunches out. Danny grabs them and swings down the aisle of the bus towards the door.

'Danny, don't be so stupid! You can't go out there. They're wolves!'

But Danny's already at the door. And I go after him. I'm frightened and shivery and excited all at once. If Danny's going to open the door, I've got to be there too. I can't let him go on his own.

'What're you going to do?'

'Chuck the food out as far as I can. Maybe they'll go off after it.' Danny puts his hand on the big metal door handle and I push up behind him. 'Go on then! What are you waiting for?'

Danny pushes the handle down hard. The door squeezes open and a flurry of snow blows into the bus so I can't see anything. Danny steps down on to the bus step and I'm beside him. Then the wind blows the other way and the snow clears and there they are. The wolves. So close I can nearly touch their rough grey-brown fur. Their hot breath smokes in the cold air. They dance as if the world belongs to them. Old wolves, young fighting wolves, she-wolves and cubs, all together in the wild falling snow. A big wolf stops and looks straight into my eyes.

'Throw the food, Danny! Throw the food!' shouts Alice behind us. 'Quick, they're going to come in the bus!'

But they're not coming in. The wolf's eyes fix on mine, big and bright and intelligent. For a second I almost believe he's going to speak to me. He's not afraid of me. And suddenly, staring back, I'm not afraid any more. I know the wolf won't hurt me. He's hungry, but it's not me he's looking for. Danny pulls back his arm and hurls the sandwiches over the wall. Instantly the wolves stream after the food. The snow closes down like a curtain and we can't see them any more.

'Shut the door! Shut the door before they come back!'

'Wait a minute.'

We strain forward, into the whirling snow. My sleeves are white with snow and the cold makes my eyes ache. I can't see anything. No rough grey-brown coats, no leaping bodies, no eyes like lamps in the gloom. I listen. Nothing. No howling from the top of the fell. Not even the sound of their paws.

'They've gone. They've really gone. It worked, Danny! They've taken the sandwiches and gone.'

'Maybe,' says Danny.

'What d'you mean?'

'What's a sandwich to a wolf? They've been gone a long time. There aren't any wolves in England any more. They're extinct.'

'What do you mean?'

'They're all dead. They've been dead for hundreds of years.'

'They can't be. We've just seen them,' says Alice. 'You saw the way they went after our sandwiches, Danny Armstrong.'

I think of the wolf that looked back at me. I saw his warm red mouth and his breath that went into the air like smoke. He was as real as me – wasn't he?

'*Wolf weather*,' I whisper. 'That's why they came. They've never really gone. They were just waiting for wolf weather so they could come back home.'

But Alice and Danny don't hear me.

'Brrr, I'm freezing,' says Alice. 'Let's shut the door.'

The door shuts and we're back in the school bus. The same boring school bus as ever, except that it'll never be quite the same. When I shut my eyes I can still see the wolves.

'What about John Johnson? Do you think they've eaten him?' asks Alice.

'You wish,' says Danny. 'He'll be back as soon as it stops snowing. We won't even miss much school. Here, have a sherbet lemon.'

He hands us the bag. Alice looks at me and I try not to laugh. This is the first time in human history that Danny Armstrong's ever shared his sweets, and it's taken a pack of wolves to make him do it. But then, in wolf weather anything can happen.

Great-grandma's Dancing Dress

Rosa coloured in the birthday card as fast as she could. She was supposed to be drawing a map of a Roman town, and any second now Mrs Hayes would come round to see how everyone was getting on. Red for the tulips, brown and yellow for the basket. What colour for the ribbon? Blue. Deep glossy blue. But Rosa hadn't got a dark blue pencil.

'Charmaine!' she whispered.

'What?'

'Can I borrow your dark blue?'

'What're you doing?' Charmaine twisted round. Her sharp green eyes lit on the card. 'Who's that for?'

'It's a birthday card for my great-grandma,' said Rosa. She knew she might as well tell Charmaine straight away, because she always found out things in the end.

'Let's have a look.' Charmaine snatched up the card. 'It's brilliant, Rosa!' she said in a voice as sweet as ice cream. But Rosa knew that voice. Charmaine fixed Rosa with eyes like magnets. 'Do one for me, Rosa. Go on. It's my mum's birthday next week.'

That was true, Rosa knew it. Her mum and Charmaine's mum were nurses in the same hospital, and Rosa and Charmaine had gone to the same child minder, the same nursery and then the same school. Year after year Charmaine sat next to Rosa. Rosa never had to find a partner for gym or dancing or walking up to the school field, because Charmaine was always there.

Sometimes Rosa wondered what it would be like to choose someone else, but she never dared. Charmaine's green eyes would snap and she would say horrible things to Rosa, the kind of things that only someone who knows you really well can say. Charmaine knew that Rosa was frightened of rats. Once Charmaine said a rat had come out of the sewers and got into Rosa's garden. For two whole weeks Rosa could not go into the garden, even though it was the hottest time of the summer and her grandma had just bought her a tent. At last she told Mum, and Mum said it wasn't true about the rat. Lots of the things Charmaine said weren't true, but Rosa never knew which ones.

'I'll give you my Disneyland rubber if you do,' said Charmaine.

'OK,' said Rosa slowly, though she didn't want the Disneyland rubber. Now Charmaine would tell her mum she'd made the card, when it was really Rosa.

Charmaine beamed. 'Here you are. Only don't use it too much,' she said, handing Rosa her dark blue glossy coloured pencil. Charmaine's pencils always looked brand new. Probably because she never does any drawing, thought Rosa. She began to colour in the numerals. Red for the 9, dark blue for the 2. *Happy Birthday, 92 today*. She shaded the colour in carefully, slowly, until it was perfect.

'Hurry up,' said Charmaine, 'you'll never get mine done if you go as slow as that.' Out of the corner of her eye Rosa saw Mrs Hayes stand up. She slid the birthday card under her folder, and bent over her Roman map. It was quite good, but the shading was smudged where Charmaine's elbow had rubbed it. As soon as Mrs Hayes had gone back to her desk after looking at everyone's map, Charmaine shoved a folded piece of white drawing paper in front of Rosa. 'Go on, quick!' she said, and Rosa began on the card for Charmaine.

The next day it was Great-grandma's birthday. But there wasn't going to be a birthday celebration, because Mum and Grandma were both working. Instead, they were going to bake a cake and have a birthday tea for Great-grandma on Saturday. But Rosa thought it was horrible for her great-grandma not to have anything on her proper birthday, even though she was so old she probably didn't care much about birthdays any more. Maybe Rosa could take the card round after school. Then she remembered that she'd already said she'd go to Charmaine's house.

Perhaps Charmaine won't mind, thought Rosa hopefully, but she knew Charmaine would. At break-time she gave Charmaine half her Milky Way, and while Charmaine's mouth was full she said quickly, 'Listen, Charmaine, you know it's my great-grandma's birthday? Well, she's on her own till Grandma comes back from work, so I thought I'd take her my card after school and say "Happy Birthday".' Charmaine swallowed the Milky Way in one gulp.

'You're coming round to my house,' she said. Her eyes bored into Rosa.

'I know. But – but can't I come tomorrow instead?'

'*Can't I come tomorrow*?' imitated Charmaine in a squeaky, pathetic little voice. 'I haven't *asked* you to come tomorrow. I asked you to come *today*, and you said yes, so now you've got to come.'

Rosa felt herself go red. 'It's only because it's her birthday.'

'I know it's her *birthday*. You've already told me that about a million times. Listen, Rosa, we're going to do something really good at my house. Mum said if we were careful we could make ice cream in her new ice cream maker. Chocolate ice cream.'

Rosa opened her mouth. She was going to do what Charmaine wanted. It was like slipping down a slide she'd slid down hundreds of times before. It was so easy. Then she thought of the card she'd made. The red tulips, the blue ribbon. And Great-grandma sitting watching TV just as she always did, as if it wasn't her birthday at all.

'I'm sorry, Charmaine,' she said, 'but I think I should go and see her. She's on her own and she's really old and –'

Charmaine leaned forward until her face was only a few inches from Rosa's. 'I know she's really old. And she's really stupid. She's a deaf stupid old bat and I hope she dies before she has another birthday and you make another stupid birthday card for her. And you needn't think I'm going to be your friend any more, because I'm not. *And* you're never coming round to my house again.' Charmaine did not shout. She never shouted. Her voice just got colder and snakier, and her fingers pinched hard into Rosa's arm. Then she gave Rosa a push and walked off.

The rest of the day Charmaine didn't speak to Rosa. She looked at her a lot, and giggled as if there was something funny about Rosa. When the bell rang Rosa went to her drawer to get the birthday card for her great-grandma. It wasn't in the blue folder. It wasn't in the plastic folder where Rosa kept her school library book. It wasn't with Rosa's other drawings. The birthday card had gone. Rosa looked through everything one more time, but she knew it was no good. Charmaine had taken the card, but she would never, ever admit it. Rosa knew what would happen. In about a week, when they were friends again, when Great-grandma's birthday was over, Charmaine would find the card. 'Oh look, Rosa, here's your birthday card! It was in your drawer all the time. You can't have looked properly.'

Rosa knelt by her drawer. Nearly everyone had gone. Only Maxine was still by the drawers, putting her homework into her bag. She gave Rosa a quick little smile. 'You OK, Rosa?'

'Yeah. I've lost something, that's all.'

Maxine hesitated. Then she said, 'I've got gymnastics, or I'd stay and help you look.'

'I didn't know you went to gymnastics,' said Rosa. She'd always wanted to do gymnastics.

'It's brilliant. I've been going to the gym centre since the beginning of term. You ought to try it, you'd be good.' Maxine did up the top of her bag. 'See you tomorrow, Rosa.' But she didn't walk off straight away. Instead she said, a bit shyly, 'You can come with me and watch next week if you want. See if you like it.'

Maxine was nice. Rosa wondered why she'd never talked to her like this before. But then on a normal day Rosa would have already left with Charmaine.

Great-grandma's room was dark except for the flickering light of the TV. She was sitting in her chair with her eyes closed.

'It's me! Happy Birthday, Great-grandma!' shouted Rosa.

It wasn't rude to shout at Great-grandma, because if you didn't she never heard anything. Slowly, Great-grandma opened her eyes. She pressed the remote control that lay on her knee and the TV screen went dark.

'Open the curtains, child, and let the sun in.'

'It isn't sunny, Great-grandma, it's raining.'

'Never mind. Rain is good for farmers,' said Great-grandma. She had lived in the city for sixty years but she still thought about farmers.

'I made you a card,' said Rosa, 'but it got lost. I'm really sorry.'

'You tell me about it. You tell me good enough and I'll see it.'

Great-grandma didn't speak the same as other people, because until she was twenty and came to England she'd never spoken one word of English.

'There were tulips, red tulips with beautiful pale green leaves, all in a basket. And I drew a dark blue ribbon round the basket. It was really good.'

'I see it now. So how come you lost such a beautiful thing?'

Rosa knelt down by Great-grandma's chair and fiddled with the remote control.

'I think,' she said, 'I think somebody took it.'

'Somebody jealous of your so-beautiful drawing,' said Great-grandma. Rose was glad Charmaine wasn't here to laugh at the way Great-grandma talked.

'Yes,' she said.

'Hmm,' said Great-grandma. Her little bony hand pushed the hair back from Rosa's forehead and she looked into Rosa's face. Rosa looked back. People always said that Rosa looked like her great-grandma, but Rosa could never believe it. Great-grandma was so old. Her face was cracked all over with lines, like a piece of dried-up earth. But her black, bright eyes were not so old. Maybe those eyes were a little bit like the eyes Rosa saw in the mirror.

'Did you ever do gymnastics?' asked Rosa. 'When you were young?'

'Gymnastics! Never. It would have been forbidden.'

'Why?'

'Many things were forbidden when I was young, especially for us girls. I will tell you something. When I was a girl I had a new blue dress, a beautiful dress, the best I ever had. My mother made it for me because she knew I wanted a dancing dress. I wanted to go to the dance in our village. I wanted that more than I ever wanted anything. Just to go and dance with my friends. I begged my father to let me go, but he took my dress and put it under his mattress and lay on his bed on top of it and he went to sleep. And I had no other dress. Already I could hear the music from the hall where the dance had begun.'

'So you couldn't go,' said Rosa.

'Oh, couldn't I?'

Rosa looked at Great-grandma's face. She was smiling. Her dark sharp eyes were snapping in her wrinkled face.

'I'll tell you the rest of the story,' she said. 'When my father was asleep and snoring, my mother put her finger on her lips and we tiptoed into the bedroom. It was dark. My mother stood on one side of the bed and I stood on the other. Then both together we lifted the mattress a tiny tiny bit and my mother pulled out the dress. And I went dancing in it. I knew my father would beat me if he found out, but he never did. He snored all night and we put the dress back under the mattress when I came home.'

Rosa thought of the big, angry father snoring on the mattress. 'You must have been frightened when you went into his room,' she said.

'Oh yes, I was frightened. My heart thumped so loud I was sure he would hear it and wake up. And my mother was frightened too. But sometimes you have to be brave, or you never do anything in your life.'

'I'll make you another card, Great-grandma,' promised Rosa. 'It'll be even better this time. I'll bring it tomorrow.' But Great-grandma did not seem to hear. She was getting tired. She smiled at Rosa then she switched on the TV and shut her eyes again. Rosa tiptoed out of the room.

The next morning Rosa was hanging up her jacket in the

school cloakroom when Charmaine came in.

'That chocolate ice cream I made last night,' said Charmaine, hanging her jacket next to Rosa's, 'was *delicious*. It was the best ice cream I've ever tasted.'

'Good,' said Rosa.

'What's the matter with *you*?' asked Charmaine. 'It was only a joke, what I said about your great-grandma. Can't you take a joke?'

Rosa fumbled in the pocket of her jacket, pretending she was looking for something. Her heart was banging. She was afraid that if she said anything her voice would be squeaky and pathetic, like the voice Charmaine imitated. Charmaine was staring at her. Rosa took a handkerchief out of her jacket pocket, as if that was what she'd been looking for. Then, just as if nothing had happened, Charmaine said, 'You can come to my house after school if you want. Since you didn't come yesterday.'

Rosa took a deep breath. 'I'm sorry,' she said. 'I'm going to my great-grandma's again. I have to take her another birthday card. The one I made yesterday got lost.'

'You don't have to,' said Charmaine. Her voice was sweet and friendly. *She knows where my birthday card is*, Rosa told herself.

Charmaine smiled confidently, as if she already knew that Rosa would do as she said. 'You don't have to go round to your great-grandma's. It's not her birthday any more.'

Suddenly Rosa did not see Charmaine. She saw her great-grandma, and her great-great-grandma, standing on each side of a mattress where a big, heavy man was snoring. She saw them lift up the mattress, and pull out her great-grandma's dancing dress.

'*Sometimes,*' said her great-grandma's voice, '*you have to be brave, or you never do anything in your life.*' Rosa took another deep breath. She seemed to see her great-grandma's eyes watching her. Great-grandma's eyes were young, though the rest of her was old. She was waiting to see what Rosa would do.

'I can't come to your house today, Charmaine,' said Rosa. Then she turned and walked out of the cloakroom. Her back felt as if it was burning where Charmaine stared after her. In the classroom there was Maxine, taking stuff out of her bag.

'How was gymnastics?' asked Rosa.

'It was great. Are you going to come next week?'

'Yes,' said Rosa, 'I think I will. Thanks, Maxine.' Then she went to her drawer, and took out her coloured pencils to begin a new birthday card for her great-grandma.

A Gap in the Dark

'*Com-ing*!'

'Cheat! She *never* counts up to twenty!' hissed Matthew as we skidded across the polished hall. No one was around to stop us, so we went up the stairs three at a time, never mind the noise. Anne was slow. She'd still be in the kitchen asking Eliza, 'Did you see them? Which way did they go? You've got to tell me!'

We raced along the gallery, and nearly cannoned into Mistress Bowman, who was carrying a heap of linen from one of the bedrooms. I slowed down and curtsied politely, but she frowned and said, 'Not so fast, Judith. Matthew, surely you should be at your studies.'

She was looking at me coldly. Perhaps she thought I was stopping Matthew from working at his Latin? No, it was more than that. She'd changed. She never smiled at me any more, or asked after my parents. Perhaps she didn't like me coming to the Hall? But I hadn't got time to think about that.

'In here,' said Matthew, and pushed me into a small

bare room. I'd never been there before. It was square, with panelled walls, and there was only a little white bed in the corner, and a candlestick on the floor beside it. The room was right at the end of the passage. If Anne came we weren't going to get away. I looked out of the window, but it was much too high for us to climb down over the roof. And there was Anne again: 'I'm com-ing. I know where you are!'

She didn't, of course. She always said that. She was still down in the hall, from the sound of it. But what was Matthew doing, feeling along the panels, pressing, stopping, pressing again? His hands looked like Blind Thomas' hands when he tapped his way through our village. A dark gap slid into place where the wall was. A hole. What was it? Matthew shoved me forward.

'Quick! Get in!'

I stepped over the threshold and into the hole. I couldn't see much and I held my hands out, feeling for the wall. There was nothing but cool, empty, black space. Matthew bent down and pulled something. Very smoothly and quickly the door slid shut. Black, velvety darkness covered me like a mask. I couldn't see my fingers. I couldn't see anything. I took a step back but the floor seemed to swing under me and I was afraid I'd fall. Matthew whispered, 'She'll never find us now.'

He was so near I could feel his warmth. It wasn't so bad

with both of us, close together, but I'd have hated to be shut in there on my own. The darkness was stifling, not like night dark or any dark I've ever known. I strained my eyes and red blobs floated in front of them.

'Where are we?' I whispered.

'Ssh, she's coming.'

We heard Anne. First of all the door banged open and there was a triumphant shout of, 'Got you!' which trailed off into, 'Judith? Matthew? I *know* you're in here. You're only teasing me, I shall tell Mother.'

She moved round the room. She must have been just the other side of the panelling, so close we could have touched her, but for the wood in our way. Everything went silent, but I felt she was still there, perhaps listening for us. Then very slowly and disappointedly her feet went away.

'She's gone.'

'I wish we had a candle.'

'There's nothing much to see. Just a cell, then the passage goes right back.'

'How strange. You wouldn't expect to find anything like this in a new building.'

Bowman Hall was built fifteen years ago, by Matthew's father. It was the finest house for miles around.

'My father had the hole put in,' said Matthew. 'It was done on purpose.'

'Why?'

'In case anyone ever needed to hide. No one knows about it. Only my mother and father, and me, and you. And perhaps Eliza does.'

'And the builders.'

'No. Only one man worked on the hole. My father trusted him.'

I didn't like talking without being able to see Matthew's face. We found ourselves whispering, even though we knew Anne had gone. The darkness pressed down on me.

'Let's get out. I'm sure she's gone.'

Matthew moved and I heard a tiny click, the sort a well-oiled lock makes. Then a slice of white appeared, like a slice of cake. It hurt my eyes. We stumbled out of the hole, blinking, and Matthew quickly closed up the panel again. You couldn't see a trace of the door once it was shut, no matter how closely you looked. Then we heard Mistress Bowman's voice calling, 'Matthew! Matthew!'

She sounded angry. Anne must have said we'd tricked her and run away. We often did. It was Anne who wanted to play hide-and-seek, not us.

'I must go home,' I said quickly, before anyone else could suggest it.

'Judith. You won't tell anyone, will you? It's very important.'

'Course I won't. I've never told on you, have I?'

I saw suddenly how important it was to Matthew. He looked older, and serious.

'Listen,' I said, 'I'm your friend. Of course I'll keep it secret.'

'Because one day . . . one day we might need to use it.'

That was the last time I was asked to visit Matthew at the Hall. After that everything changed. We had to meet down by the river, or in the woods where no one saw us. My mother kept me busy milking and churning with my sister Becky. When I said I wanted to see Matthew she frowned, the way Mistress Bowman had done.

'You're to keep away from the Bowmans now, Judith. These are dangerous times for friendships between them and us. Don't you know they follow the old religion? You know what that means?'

I nodded. I did know. I'd heard it all round the village. Papists were dangerous. They wanted to kill our Queen and bring the King of Spain here to rule over us. There were plots everywhere. We'd have good men burned alive at Smithfield again, the way it was under Bloody Mary. Ours was a good Protestant village, loyal to the Queen. That was what they said, but I knew it couldn't all be true. After all, Matthew was my friend and I noticed that my mother and father never joined in when such things were said. I looked at my mother. Her face was anxious. Afraid. Afraid for me, the way she used to be when I went too near the fire when I was little.

'You must tell Matthew you have work to do at home. It's true enough.'

'The Bowmans are our neighbours, Susannah,' said my father.

'Don't you let anyone hear you talking like that, John. Don't you know that there are Government spies everywhere, even in our village?'

A look passed between my parents. A look I couldn't understand. There was a secret, and I was shut out of it.

Suddenly it seemed as if everyone in our village was whispering about the Bowmans. People said a woman had been executed in York for hiding a Papist priest. Margaret something, her name was. Everyone was afraid. It's hard to describe what it was like. The whispering was like a shadow which covered everything and got in everywhere. What if the Bowmans were plotting? What if they were hiding priests? Would they bring down the government spies and torturers on us all? My mother listened, but I noticed that she never said a word. She didn't smile any more, either, and there was a new line on her forehead, between her eyes.

I was taking a basket of eggs down the village street when I first saw the man. He was on a fine mare, but she was worn out and sweating, with a white lather on her flanks. He was a gallant in a feathered hat and a velvet cloak, but he was covered in dust and dirt as if he'd come a long way, riding hard. He slowed the mare beside me and I could smell the heat of her. She was trembling and her flanks were going in and out, quickly. I knew she could not go on more than another mile.

'Is there a tavern here where I can rest myself and the mare?' he called.

'Joe Barraclough will serve you, sir. You'll find him outside the tavern.'

Joe was always outside the tavern, lounging and drinking ale in the sun while his wife cooked and served and wiped and cleaned. Still, he'd feed and groom the mare. He was good with horses.

'Thank you,' said the man. He smiled at me, and I noticed how warm his smile was, not at all like the gallants in York who'd as soon ride their horses' hooves over your feet as slow down for you. Then suddenly his smile froze. He stared at me. His eyes widened, almost as if he recognised me, as if he was about to say my name.

'Who are you?' he asked, in a small dry voice. His throat must have been full of dust.

'My name is Judith, sir. Judith Hestone.'

He let his breath out in a sigh. 'Ah. Hestone. Of course.' His hands were tight on the reins. The mare shivered, then put her head down and nuzzled my hand. I was burning with questions. Why 'Of course'? Why did he seem to know me?

'Joe Barraclough's tavern,' he said, as if remembering something a long way back. 'I must go there now. Goodbye, Judith,' and he walked the mare on, leaving me looking after him.

It was not so long afterwards that I saw a knot of people coming up to our door. That wasn't unusual. People often came to talk to father about disputes and troubles, because he could usually calm them down and find an answer. I loitered round to listen.

'You know that fine gallant in the tavern . . .'

'I swear he's not what he seems . . .'

'Joe found a box in his saddle-bag . . .'

'Evil doings – he's got a prayer book with him, full of Papish prayers . . .'

'Look at his face. And the way he limps. He's no gallant. He's a priest for sure, dressed up to fox us . . .'

'And where's he going, I should like to know?'

'Bowmans! Bowman Hall for sure!'

'Bowmans!'

They all took it up, their faces red and glistening. Father couldn't calm them this time. My mother stood beside him, her face white and frantic, arguing against the people. They wouldn't listen to her either. First they wanted to seize the man at once, and tie him up in Joe Barraclough's stable until the queen's men could get here. Then another said we ought to pretend nothing was amiss and let him go on up to Bowman Hall. We'd ride for the queen's soldiers and they'd catch him up there and catch the Bowmans too, for sheltering a Papist priest. *We'll do this*, they said. *No, we'll do that.*

I stood there, feeling cold, looking at faces. There was Simon Tolliver, who rented two fields from the Bowmans. He always said the rent was too high.

'We'll lead the soldiers to Bowmans!' he shouted.

We. I was in the crowd, part of it. But was I? Matthew was my friend, more than anyone else in the village. Matthew trusted me.

'Did I ever tell on you?' I'd said. I'd told him I could keep a secret. I was his friend. I didn't have to do anything to betray Matthew. All I had to do was to do nothing and stand there, part of the crowd. My friend. Matthew. I saw his face in front of me, the way it was once, white and sick because he'd hit a trout's head on a stone to kill it and it wouldn't stop flapping. I'd taken the slippery thing from him and struck it on the stone again. I never minded things like that.

I slipped back slowly out of the crowd so no one would see me go. My heart was banging. They would capture the Bowmans, Matthew and Anne and all his family. And what would they do to them? I'd heard of people being questioned, put on the rack to make them talk. Better not think about it.

I went round the back of our house, keeping close to the hedge, then through the gate into the pastures. This way I could go across country to Bowman Hall. It wasn't more than a mile from the village, and I could run. I could run Becky to a standstill any day, and even Matthew couldn't beat me. Joe Barraclough would let the priest go off on horseback to Bowmans, round by the lane, thinking that no one suspected him. I would cut across and be able to warn him before he reached the house. How long would it take to fetch the queen's men? Not long. There were soldiers quartered at Riddal.

I'm a good runner, but every breath burned and my legs were shaking as I reached the top of the lane and flopped down on the verge. I couldn't hear anything. Had the priest passed already? No. There it was, the faint picking noise of hooves. In a few minutes he came round the corner of the lane, going slower than ever. He was urging the mare on,

'Come on, good girl, Bess . . .'

I stood up slowly so as not to frighten the mare or the man. He stopped, looking surprised.

'You're wandering far from home, Judith.'

It might have been because I'd been running, but I couldn't speak properly. I panted, 'They're getting the queen's men. They know who you are. I came to warn you.'

His eyes went wide and still. The mare trembled all over as if she felt something.

'How long will it take till they get here?'

'I don't know. Not more than an hour. They've only to go to Riddal, and they've taken horses.'

'I'll have to leave the mare. Go across country . . .' He was thinking aloud.

'No!' I said. 'You'll be caught. You can't hide in those clothes.'

Than I remembered the hole, and what Matthew had said. *'One day we might need to use it.'*

One day was now. I mustn't tell the priest about it yet, in case we were caught before we got to the Hall. He might give away the Bowmans' secret, if they tortured him. People did.

'There's a place. A hiding place up at the Hall.'

Then he asked me a question I didn't understand then. 'Did your mother send you?'

'No, she doesn't know anything about it. Quick, we've got to hurry!'

'I'll leave the mare here,' he said. 'Better if they think I've run off into the woods. Poor old girl, poor Bess, will you fend for yourself?'

'She's a fine mare. Someone'll take her, and be glad of her,' I said.

He slid off the saddle, and stood wearily on the lane. I

could see how stiff his legs were. The mare put her head down and began to graze. He undid his saddlebag and slung it on his back. It looked strange on top of his rich cloak. He walked so slowly, limping.

'Quick!' I said. 'Men from the village will come up to guard the lanes while others fetch the soldiers.'

He hobbled along, not at all like a fine gentleman.

'Can't you go faster?' I begged.

He laughed quietly, as if it didn't matter at all. 'I had a taste of the rack once,' he said. 'They let me go that time, but it's left a mark on my bones.'

And yet he was still going round the country, dodging and hiding, even though he knew what would happen if they caught him.

'You could take my arm,' I said.

We went as fast as we could, him hobbling and leaning on me. My shoulder ached from his weight. If only he'd left the saddlebag, we'd have got on better, but when I suggested he hide it in a ditch he gasped out, 'No. That's why I'm here.' I knew he must have his priestly things in the bag, and I didn't complain about it any more.

The Hall was very quiet. We came in the back way, through the stable yard, with the doves bubbling and cooing, and Matthew's mare Star looking over her stable door at us. I pushed open the kitchen door and there was Eliza. She was stirring milk over the fire, and she turned and saw us.

'What's this, Judith? You know you're not supposed to come here –'

'Quick. He's a priest. The queen's men are coming. The men from the village are fetching them. They want to trap the Bowmans.'

'God have mercy on us, and Mistress Bowman's sick with an ague. I was making this posset for her. And the master's away.' She held out the mixture of milk and honey as if it would solve everything.

'Where's Matthew?' I said. At least he'd help me do something. Then Eliza changed. Her big body became purposeful. Calling for Matthew she steered us through the kitchen. A door upstairs opened and I heard Matthew clattering down.

'Where's Anne?' I asked. 'She mustn't see us.'

'Now, where's Miss Anne? Ah, she's in the orchard, picking up eggs. The hens are laying astray again.'

Possets, hens, eggs. Was that all Eliza could think of?

'Matthew!'

It didn't take more than a minute to explain to Matthew. It was strange. It seemed as if he was prepared for this. Almost as if he'd been waiting for it.

'He was going to go off cross-country but I brought him here because of the secret place,' I said, and Matthew nodded. His freckles stood out, the way they did when he was angry. He bowed to the priest.

'Father,' he said, 'you are very welcome here. We'll have to get him upstairs, Judith.'

Together we helped the priest up the stairs. We had to hurry. At the top I looked back and saw the dusty treads we'd left across Eliza's polished floor.

'Eliza! Wipe off all the marks. They'll see where we've gone.'

We looked out of the low passage window, where the window seat was. Matthew and I used to sit there on rainy days, telling stories and eating Eliza's honeycakes. There was the orchard. There was Anne in her blue dress, bending down and searching the long grass for eggs. And there, beyond Anne . . . Two heads. At the orchard wall. They bobbed, then looked up, and over. We sank out of sight, but I'd recognised them.

'Sammy Orr and Ben Striddle.'

'What about Anne? They'll frighten her.'

'She doesn't know anything and anyone can tell that she doesn't. You can't call her in now.'

We were in the little square room again. It was hot with the sun pouring into it. The priest let go of our shoulders and straightened himself. Matthew was already feeling the panels, trying to find the catch. His hands were clumsy, but at last the panel slid and darkness appeared. The priest raised his hand. I didn't know what he was doing at first, then he made the sign of the cross. He was blessing us.

'Food!' I said. 'Have we got time?'

'They're watching the house. And Anne might come in and see me carrying it up. We haven't got time.'

No food or drink then. Just darkness. The priest stepped carefully over the threshold.

'Pass me my bag,' he said. 'Gently . . . What's in that bag is more important than I am.'

'Matthew,' I said, 'I'll have to go in with him.'

He frowned. I could almost see his thoughts pass over his face. 'But it might be days, Judith. When the queen's men get here they'll search the house but they won't leave straight away. If they suspect there's a priest-hole they'll camp here and try to starve him out.'

'I can't leave now. They'll see me. They'll know I've come from the village to warn you. They know I'm your friend. They might burn the house down.'

It had been done to other houses. We both knew it.

'I'll bring you food. I swear it. Three scratches on the door and it'll be me. There's water in a pitcher just inside the panel, on your left.'

'But why? I mean, how did you know?'

'It's always there. Just in case . . .'

Just in case. We looked at each other, then I stepped forward and the panel slid shut behind me. Darkness moved all over me like velvet, like something alive. I could hear the priest's breathing, harsh and laboured, close to me.

'Move back,' I said. 'The passage goes back.'

We edged back, back, back, until we struck cold stone wall. There was a dank smell, as if the air had been here for a long time, never changing or blowing away. It made me shiver. He must have felt it because he said in a murmur which you couldn't have heard more than three feet away, 'Don't be afraid.'

Don't be afraid! He was the one who ought to be afraid. Or perhaps I was too. After all, I was hiding a priest. Betraying the people of my own village. Helping a priest to safety. That's what they'd say – 'How could you do it, Judith?'

Bloody Mary. Bonfires at Smithfield. Bringing back the Papists. The King of Spain ruling over England. But it wasn't like that. Matthew was a Papist, and I was a Protestant, but we were friends. That felt more important than anything. And I could tell from his breathing that the priest was in pain. And what would they have done to him if they'd caught him?

We waited. My breathing was jerky and my heart banged until I couldn't tell if I was hearing footsteps or not. Then at last we felt them. The crash of heavy boots vibrating through the house, shaking the floor, coming closer and closer. I'd never heard footsteps like those in any house, footsteps which didn't care what noise they made, what damage they did. The air seemed to shake with them. Thick, dark, shaking air pressed against my face, filling my ears and my eyes and my mouth. Voices shouted, loud outdoor voices, angry, echoing from room to room. They didn't belong in this house. Then a crash, and a cry, and another crash as if something had been flung against the panelling. Or someone. They were in the room, just the other side of the wooden wall. I was shaking – or was it the priest shaking? Was it my hand slippery with sweat, or his? I didn't care. It didn't matter.

Then the batter of noise stopped. Everything was quiet as the inside of a grave. I knew they were listening. Listening for us. Waiting for us to give ourselves away by a cough or a whisper. Then more shouting, more footsteps, but going away from us now. I followed them in my mind, across the room, through the door, down the polished gallery.

A murmur in my ear. The priest.

'Don't stir. It's a trick. To make us think they've gone.'

I couldn't stand up any longer. I slid down to the floor and crouched there. I tried to shut my mind but I kept hearing things, remembering things:

'. . . that woman executed in York . . . Margaret something . . . two priests hanged at Tyburn, they say . . . took them in for questioning . . . put them on the rack . . . they soon talked . . .'

They would torture the priest to make him talk. Would they torture me? If they asked me questions, would I be able to stop myself answering them? We crouched in the dark, side by side, peering into nothing.

'You're a brave girl,' the priest whispered. Then he added in a low voice, so low I was hardly sure if I'd heard it or not, 'Like your mother.'

'Like Mother? What do you mean? Do you know Mother?'

'You're old enough to keep a secret, Judith?'

Here we were, hiding in the dark from the queen's men who might kill us if they found us, and he was asking me if I was old enough to keep a secret? He must have realised how stupid it was, because he said, 'I'm sorry. Of course you are. Yes, I knew your mother long ago, when we were children. That's how I knew who you were. You're very like her. Then we grew up and she married your father and came here, and I went abroad.'

'She never told me anything about you.'

'Perhaps she thought it was best not.'

My mother seemed like a different person suddenly. She'd had friends I'd never even known she had. And they grew up together. He must have been important to her. But he became a priest. I had so many questions to ask –

Three scratches, and then the white gap in the dark. It hurt my eyes again. Matthew's voice.

'Quick. Over here.'

We stumbled towards the light. Matthew pushed past me and shoved a basket and a bundle into the hole, then hauled me out. The priest let go of my hand. I looked back, but he didn't move. I could see his face in the light from the panel door before Matthew shut it again and left him there alone.

'Hurry. We can get you out. All the women and children from the village are up here, round the house. They came with the soldiers. They're making sure no one escapes. Go straight down the stairs and into the kitchen. There's a guard on the main door but if anyone sees you, say you pushed your way in. If you curse us and yell enough they'll believe you. Once you're in the stable yard you can slip into the crowd and start shouting like the rest of them. Everyone knows you.'

'I shan't do that. I shan't yell and shout like them,' I said angrily.

'You will. You've got to. Then no one'll guess.'

And I did. I cursed the Bowmans for Papists, I shook my fist and spat and swayed and yelled with the crowd. The soldiers wanted us there, but they didn't want us to get too rough. All the village was there, but my mother and father never came. When we surged forward the soldiers pushed us back, showing their pikes.

It wasn't until nightfall that some of the crowd began to get bored and drift back to the village. After all there was nothing to see. Mistress Bowman was sick with ague, and she'd been good to many in the village in her time. She'd made medicines out of herbs and sent wine to people who were sick. People began to remember it. They grew cold and shifted their feet and thought of home.

But I stayed. I stayed and watched it all. Three soldiers skewered live hens on their swords: Mistress Bowman's hens, whose eggs Anne had been hunting. Others lit a fire in the stable yard while James the stableboy looked on, not daring to protest, white with fear that the stables would catch fire and the horses burn alive. The officers watched and smiled. I saw it all.

My mother ran out to meet me as I came in through our gate. Her face was pale.

'Where have you been, Judith?'

'Up at the Hall.'

She reached out and hugged me so tight I could hear her heart bumping.

'They haven't caught him,' she whispered.

'No. He's hidden. Mother —' but I didn't go on. She hadn't told me, and it was her secret.

'All the village is up there,' I said. 'I hate them!'

'You mustn't do that,' said my mother. 'They are our neighbours. We have to live with them.'

They didn't find the priest that time. He crouched behind the panelling for three days while the soldiers sat in the kitchen and ate the hams and cheeses Eliza had put away for the winter, and drank all Mistress Bowman's mead and apple wine. At night they got drunk and roared out songs, keeping time with their fists and their boots. You could hear them all through the yard and the orchard and way down nearly to the village. From the village, people could see the fires they lit, leaping and roaring into the sky as if the Hall itself was on fire. But they didn't fire the Hall. Not this time. They smashed Mistress Bowman's fine chairs, and ripped her mattresses with their swords 'til the house was full of feathers, saying they were looking for the priest. They burned the henhouses and when they left they took Star with them and they would have taken Matthew's father's mare if she hadn't been lame. I thought of how Matthew couldn't bear to knock the head of a trout against a stone, but he had to live for three days in that house with the soldiers listening for every sound, and his mother sick and Anne whimpering with terror every time a soldier came into the room. It would keep on happening, over and over, I knew, as long as the Bowmans stayed Papist.

I saw the soldiers go. They had their packs clutched to them full of what was left of the Bowman's stores. And china, and glass, and everything they could carry. No matter if it smashed on the journey. I stood in the yard and watched the stragglers go. There were only a few of us from the village left now, and we didn't look at each other much. You might have thought we were ashamed. I listened to their boots, going off down the lane, and I stood there, watching the house. The sun was warm, and the doves which were still alive were purring up on the roof. Soon the last few watchers would go back to the village, and I would knock softly on the side-door, and Matthew would let me in.

I had scarcely been home those past three days, except to eat and to sleep, but my mother knew where I was and she didn't stop me. She understood that I wanted to be where Matthew was, even if I couldn't help him. Once or twice she started to say something and I thought she was going to tell me about the boy she had known all those years ago, who was a Papist too. But it wasn't the right time. She kept her secret and I kept mine.

The village people would say I'd betrayed them if they knew how I'd run across the fields to warn the priest and help him hide, but I knew now that my parents would be glad I'd done it. I'd kept Matthew's secret, and I could keep my mother's. I was part of it now.

Aliens Don't Eat Bacon Sandwiches

My brother Cal has been making his own bacon sandwiches since he was ten years old. It's not that he likes cooking that much, it's just that no one else knows how to make the perfect bacon sandwich.

He'd get everything ready by the cooker first. Bacon, bread, tomatoes, ketchup, sharp knife. The bacon had to be fried fast, so it was crisp but not dried up. He'd lay it on one slice of soft white bread, smear it with ketchup, cover it with tomato slices, and then clap a matching white slice on top. Then he'd bite into it while the bacon was hot and the fat was soaking into the bread. Dad used to say that Cal would go to Mars and back if he thought there'd be a bacon sandwich at the end of it. Don't forget this. The bacon sandwich is important.

Then there was the cordless phone. We should never have bought it, Mum said. I mean, I like talking to my friends on the phone, but Cal was something else. He was never off it. When he came in from school he'd pick up the phone right away and call someone he'd only been talking to half an hour before. And they'd talk and talk and talk. Sometimes Mum would come in and stand there tapping her watch or mouthing 'phone bill!' at him, but it never seemed to make any difference. Cal was a phone addict. I was cleaning my bike in the garden one day, and Mum and her friend Susie were talking about telephones and big bills and teenage kids. Susie said, 'It's all right as long as you realise that teenagers aren't people at all really. They're aliens from outer space. That's why they spend all their time on the phone. They have to keep in contact with other aliens who come from the same planet.'

I didn't take much notice of what Susie said at the time, but it came back to me later. Mum leaned back in her deck chair and laughed. She'd been out on a location all day, taking photographs – Mum's a photographer. She was working on a feature about corn circles. I expect you've seen pictures of them. Perfect circles in wheat, much too perfect to have been made by wind or rain. There were more of them than ever that year, and nobody knew how they came. At first the newspapers said it was a hoax. Reporters and photographers used to sit up and keep watch all night by cornfields, to catch the hoaxers. But they never did. Somehow they'd get sleepy and doze off and then when they jerked awake the circle would be there, just as round as if it had been drawn with a compass.

Mum could have stayed the night too. She was working with a journalist friend who'd brought a tent along. Mum talked to Cal and me about it, then she decided not to stay. It was just a feeling she had that it wasn't a good idea. Cal and I always listened to Mum when she got feelings about things. Even I could remember how she'd said to Dad, just before he went on that last trip, 'Do be careful, love. I've got a feeling about it. I wish you weren't going.'

Dad worked for Interstel airways, on the crash investigation team. He was an instrument specialist. This time he wasn't investigating a crash, but several pilots had reported interference with their instruments over the Mojave Desert. They'd managed to correct the problems manually so far, but the airline was quietly panicking. Dad had been working on a computer model, trying to find some pattern in what was going on. I don't remember much about that time, but Cal told me later that Dad had been up most of the night the week before he left. He was really worried. All he said to Cal and Mum was that a pattern kept coming up, and he didn't like the look of it.

Mum's feeling was right. Dad's plane crashed not far from Coyote Lake. Something went wrong with the instruments, they said. There'd been massive distortions caused by what looked like a powerful electrical storm. At least, that's what it looked like on the computer trace. But no storm showed up for hundreds of miles on the weather charts.

I asked Mum if she thought the corn circles really were made by aliens, like people said. She frowned, then she said, 'I don't know, Tony. I don't believe that the circles are made by UFOs landing. That would be much too obvious. The feeling I have is that we're being teased. Or tricked. As if someone – or something – is trying to distract us from what they're really doing.'

'What do you mean?'

'It's hard to explain, but try to put yourself in their place. If there really are aliens trying to get a foothold on our planet, I think they'd do it in a way we'd hardly even notice. There'd be changes, but not huge ones. After all, there are millions of us on this planet, and only a few of them. They'd come in very gradually over the years. They wouldn't want to risk being noticed – not too soon.'

'We'd be bound to notice, though, wouldn't we?'

'Not necessarily. Think of burglars. Some break in through the front door with crowbars, but others come in pairs pretending to be insurance salesmen. It's not till long after they've gone that you realise one of them's nipped upstairs and taken all your valuables. If there *were* aliens they wouldn't want to seem different. They'd want to seem like us. Part of normal life.'

So Mum thought the corn circles were there to keep us

busy, to stop us noticing what else was going on. I shivered.

Cal was fifteen and a half, and I was eleven. You wouldn't think we'd be friends as well as brothers, but we always had been. Cal told me things he'd never tell Mum. He knew I'd never grass him up. And if something made him sad he could tell me that too. He got a music centre for his fifteenth birthday, much better than the one downstairs in the sitting room. He'd lie on his bed and I'd lie on the floor and we'd listen to his music and he'd tell me about what was going on with his friends; not all of it, but some. Enough. Cal had a Saturday job, so he always had money. And he'd talk to me about Genevieve. He knew I liked her. He'd had girlfriends before, but Genevieve was different.

That was another clue I didn't pick up straight away. It was about five o'clock and Cal and I were home from school, but Mum wasn't back yet. The phone rang and I answered it. It was Genevieve. She asked how I was, the way she always did. She even remembered that I'd had to take my budgie to the vet, and asked if he was OK now. Then she said, 'Is Cal there, Tony?'

'Yes, I'll just get him.'

I turned round. Cal was lounging in the doorway, watching me.

'It's Genevieve,' I said, holding out the phone, but Cal didn't take it. He just kept on looking at me. It's hard to describe what happened next. I hadn't really been thinking about what was going on, because I was just doing something I'd done loads of times before, taking a call for Cal and passing it on to him. And since it was Genevieve I knew he'd be pleased. But he wasn't pleased this time. He didn't react at all. I felt as if I was searching Cal's face for someone who wasn't there, like you'd search an empty house for a light in the windows.

'It's *Genevieve*!' I hissed, thinking perhaps he hadn't heard, and wishing I'd pressed the silence button in case Genevieve had. But Cal just shook his head, very slightly, as if he was making fun of me. Or Genevieve. And I was left holding the phone.

'I'm sorry, Genevieve,' I gabbled, 'he just went out I think, I mean I thought he was here, but he isn't.' It must have sounded like a lie, but Genevieve isn't a suspicious sort of person.

'Oh, that's OK, Tony,' she said. 'I'll try again later. See you,' and she put the phone down. Her voice was just the same as always. You know how some people's voices make you feel that good things are about to happen? Genevieve had that sort of voice.

Cal's voice was cold and irritated. I couldn't believe I was hearing him right.

'I wish she'd stop bothering me,' he said.

'What?'

'You heard. I said I wish she'd stop bothering me. That

girl really bugs me. If she calls again, say you don't know when I'll be back. No. Never mind. I'll take the phone.'

He held his hand out for it. Darkness looked out of his eyes, and blankness. There was no Cal there at all. He took the phone and held it up as if he was going to dial straight away. The silver antenna poked out at the side of his head. I felt a shiver go through me. The antenna. Cal's dead eyes. Something scratched at the back of my mind, wanting to be let in: *'That's why they spend all their time on the phone, so they can keep in touch with all the other aliens . . .'*

I stared at Cal and he stared back at me. Mocking, as if he knew something I didn't. And in a way . . . almost frightening. And then I heard Mum's key go into the front door lock. Cal stopped looking at me. By the time Mum called hello to us, he was already on his way up the stairs, calling back 'Homework' as he went. That was strange, too. Cal usually made Mum a cup of coffee when she got in from work. His bedroom door banged with the sort of bang that tells everyone else to keep out. I waited to hear the music. Cal always turned on his music as soon as he got into his room. But nothing happened. It was absolutely silent, as if there was no Cal in there at all.

That was the first evening Cal didn't eat supper. He'd been into Burger King with Alex on his way back from school. Mum didn't bother about it. She was tired and upset because she and her journalist friend had had an argument with their editor. The editor didn't like the idea of aliens coming in secretly while we were all busy with the corn circles. He wasn't going to run the feature unless they changed it. The next day Cal said he had to finish a piece of coursework and could he take a sandwich and a glass of milk up to his room. I don't remember all the excuses for not eating after that, at breakfast and tea and supper. They were never the same twice.

Cal had always been clever, but now he was cunning too. He emptied his wastepaper basket every day, so there was no chance of Mum finding the sandwiches he hadn't eaten. It was hard to know how much Mum had noticed. She never said anything, and she carried on giving Cal dinner money as usual.

It was three nights after the phone call to Genevieve that I couldn't sleep. My bedroom was next to Cal's, but I hadn't been into Cal's room for three days. Have you ever seen two magnets fighting one another with an invisible force field between them? There was one of those force fields at Cal's bedroom door. You couldn't see it, you couldn't touch it, but it was there. Even Mum found excuses not to go in there. She was collecting the dirty washing one afternoon when Cal was late home, and she said, 'I ought to have a sock search under Cal's bed,' but she didn't go in. She hesitated by his door, then she said, 'No. He's old enough to sort out his own dirty washing,' and she walked past into my room to change my duvet cover.

I kept turning over and over in bed. I was used to falling asleep to the sound of Cal's music, and I couldn't settle down in the silence. What was he doing? Was he just sitting there? Reading? Working? I knew there wasn't anyone else in his room, though usually Cal had his friends round a lot, and often they stayed late. None of his friends had been round for the past three days. And I don't know what he'd said to Genevieve, but she hadn't called again. I tossed back the duvet and it flumped on to the floor. I found myself tiptoeing across the carpet, easing the door handle down, pulling the door open very gently. The landing light was on. Everything was quiet and Mum's door was shut too. 12.37 on my watch. She'd be asleep.

My heart thudded as I crept close to Cal's door. Yes, it was still there, the invisible hand pushing me away, saying I wasn't wanted there. But I wasn't going to take any notice this time. This was Cal, my brother. I took a breath, and touched his door handle. Something fizzed on my fingers, like a tiny electric charge, like a rush of static electricity. I pulled my hand away and stepped back. Then I stopped myself.

'It's only Cal,' I told myself fiercely, 'it's only Cal.'

This time the prickle of electricity wasn't so bad, or perhaps it was OK because I was expecting it. Very gently I pushed the handle down. It didn't squeak or click. Then I pushed the door. As it opened, a narrow strip of light fell from the landing into the darkness of Cal's room. It lit up Cal's bed, which was opposite the door. It lit up Cal, who was sitting up on the bed, fully dressed, reading. Reading in the dark. It lit up Cal's eyes as he turned to me, not at all surprised, as if he'd been expecting me. As if he'd seen me through the door.

'Hi,' he said, and turned a page.

There was only one switch for the main light, and it was by the door. It was off. I opened the door wider, so that more light came in, and walked across to Cal's bed. Casually, I touched his bedside light. It was cold. It hadn't been on at all. He'd really been reading in the dark – unless he'd been pretending? Unless he was trying to trick me and he'd been sitting there with the book, waiting for me to come in? But then how had he known I was going to come in? There wasn't an answer. There was only Cal sitting on his bed. He didn't look as if he liked me much.

'I can't sleep,' I said. 'I'm going down to make some hot chocolate. Do you want some?'

'No,' said Cal. A week ago he'd have come down with me so I wouldn't make too much noise and wake up Mum. He'd have whipped up the chocolate, the way he does. Suddenly I had an idea.

'I'm going to make a bacon sandwich,' I said, and waited for Cal to say what he always said, 'You make a bacon sandwich? Don't make me laugh. Let the man from the army do it.' And then he'd make it for me.

He didn't. But something went over his face. Just for a second, there was a flicker of the real Cal, and as soon as I saw it I knew for sure that whoever else had been there the past three days, it hadn't been Cal. Then his face went back to the not-Cal face. The alien face. I felt the back of my neck prickle. Maybe it was the electricity, tingling around the room. Out of the corner of my eye I caught a movement. It was the minute hand of Cal's electric wall clock, racing crazily round and round. The thing inside my brother looked straight at me, daring me to say what I'd seen. The prickle ran up my arms and down again. I'd run into a storm, just the way Dad had done, only here it wasn't as strong. There was only one of them here. I shook my head to clear the buzzing of my thoughts. Cal needed me.

'I really fancy a bacon sandwich,' I said again, 'we've got all the stuff. White bread, tomatoes, ketchup – and Mum bought some back bacon yesterday.'

Something struggled in his eyes again, like the ghost of my brother. It wasn't winning. Cal wanted so much to come back, but he couldn't. There was something else there, something alien, and it was too strong for Cal. It meant to stay, and it meant to keep Cal out of his own body. But at least now I felt I knew what I was fighting. What *we* were fighting.

Cal hadn't eaten anything for three days, I knew he hadn't. He must be hungry. Whatever was in him now didn't need food, not our earth food. But Cal did. And Cal would do anything for a bacon sandwich. Perhaps, if I could take him by surprise somehow, and get him to eat – could that break whatever power this thing had over him? I didn't know, but it was worth trying.

'See you downstairs if you change your mind,' I said.

Our neighbours have a baby which cries in the night, so Mum goes to bed with cotton wool in her ears. Even so, I moved quietly as I lit the gas, got out the heavy frying pan, found bacon and tomatoes in the fridge, rummaged in the cupboard for ketchup. I just hoped the smell of frying bacon wouldn't wake her. I put the frying pan on, melted a bit of fat, and lowered the bacon on the slice. It fizzled. After a minute the first tantalising wisp of the smell of frying bacon began to wreathe round the kitchen. Soon it would be through the door, then up the stairs, then under Cal's door. I turned up the heat carefully. I didn't want it to burn. The bacon spluttered, making a friendly sound in the kitchen. I laid the bread ready, and the sliced tomatoes, and the ketchup bottle. A drop of hot fat sparked on to the back of my hand and I sucked it away. Cal. Cal. Cal.

'Cal'd go to Mars and back if he thought he'd get a bacon sandwich at the end of it,' Dad used to say. That was before Dad went.

The kitchen door opened. Cal walked slowly, as if he was pushing through something heavy. His face was pale, and it wasn't smooth and hard any more, the way it had been the past three days. It looked crumpled, as if he was trying to remember something.

'Your sandwich is nearly ready,' I said. I took the bacon off the heat, slid the slices out of the pan and laid them across the bread. I layered on the tomato and squeezed out just the right amount of ketchup. Then I cut the sandwich in half. Cal watched me all the time. I lifted my half, and took a bite. I saw him lick his lips, but he was shivering, as if he felt cold. And things were moving behind his eyes, as if they were fighting for space there.

'Cal,' I said, 'your sandwich is getting cold.'

His hands had dropped to his sides. They looked heavy. He didn't have the strength even to lift his hands, because all his strength was going into that fight inside him, between the Cal who was my brother and the stranger who wanted to make his home inside my brother's body. And that stranger was hanging on, tooth and claw. It wasn't going to let go easily.

I knew now for sure that it was nothing human that was looking at me out of Cal's eyes. It had come from far away, and all it cared about was its resting place. It was here for a purpose. It didn't care for Cal, or me, or any of us. All it cared about was what it needed. Cal would never eat or sleep again, if it had its way.

'Cal,' I said again. It felt as if his name was all I had. I came up close to him with his half of the sandwich still in my hand. He backed off a step or two, but then he didn't go any farther. I knew it was the real Cal who wanted to stay.

Suddenly I remembered something from far back, when I was sick with tonsillitis, not long after Dad died. It was when I was about six, I think. I had to take medicine four times a day, and I hated it. I used to press my lips tight shut and Mum couldn't make me swallow it. Then Cal took the spoon. He didn't seem worried, like Mum, and he didn't have any doubt that I'd open my mouth. He just put the spoon near my lips, without trying to push it into my mouth, and he said, 'Come on, kiddo. Do it for me.' And I did, every time, four times a day till I was better. The words had been like magic to me then, when I was a little kid. Would they work now? Could they be the one thing that would bring Cal back and help him to fight off that powerful and lonely thing which had come to make its home in him?

I held the bacon sandwich up to Cal's mouth. His face was sweaty and he was breathing hard, as if he'd been running a long way.

'Come on, kiddo,' I whispered. 'Do it for me.'

I held my breath. I said it again, but silently. Then, like something in slow motion, Cal's mouth opened. I could see how hungry he was, how much he wanted to come home.

I felt the electric prickle again, the one I'd felt when I first tried to open Cal's door. It was stronger now. It was trying to beat up a storm. It was fighting me, as well as Cal. But this time it wasn't going to win. Cal bit down. He bit into the white bread, the bacon which was still hot, the juicy tomato. I saw the marks of his teeth in the bread. He chewed, and he swallowed a mouthful of the bacon sandwich. Then I looked at him and it was like looking at a house where all the lights have come on at once after it's been empty for a long time. His hands weren't heavy any more. He grasped the sandwich, bit again, and in a minute he'd finished it.

'You going to make me another, Tony, or have I got to show you how the man from the army makes a bacon sandwich?' he asked, and he smiled.

I didn't even jump when Mum opened the kitchen door. I knew it was her, not the thing which had been here and which was gone now, away through lonely space and places I couldn't begin to imagine, looking for somewhere else to make its home. Mum pulled the cotton wool out of her ears.

'You boys,' she said, 'I should have known. I was dreaming about bacon sandwiches.'

I don't know how Cal made it up with Genevieve, but the next day she was round at our house again. Cal's bedroom door was open, and his music was throbbing through the house. Mum didn't tell him to turn it down. She was in a wonderful mood because the editor had rung her back. He'd changed his mind and he was going to run the story about the corn circles in the way Mum and her friend wanted. For some reason he'd suddenly come to think it was worth printing the theory about aliens operating like bogus insurance salesmen, distracting us with corn circles and stealing our valuables when we weren't looking. I asked Mum, 'Does the editor have kids?'

'Yes, he's got a teenage daughter. She's been a bit of a problem lately, apparently – he was telling me.' Mum glanced round, saw Cal was laughing with Genevieve, and whispered, 'His daughter's been acting a bit like Cal has these past few days, I think. But he says she's got over it, too.'

Genevieve stayed to supper, and you can guess what we ate. While we were eating it I thought of what had happened the night before, in our midnight kitchen.

Aliens don't eat bacon sandwiches, I thought, looking at my brother.

A Close Match

'Oh – is she really your sister?' People are always asking me that, as if I'd bother to lie. And then they look from me to Jennifer. 'I'd never have have guessed you were sisters.'

Nor would I. I used to make up a lot of stuff about being adopted, and that was why Mum and Jennifer were tall and fair, and I was short and dark. But my dad's dark, or at least he was before he went grey, and he's half a head shorter than Mum.

'It's funny how different sisters can be, isn't it?' That's what my aunts and uncles say. But it's not all that funny for me, because the difference is that Jennifer's got everything. She has long legs that go deep brown in summer, and thick smooth hair that gets blonde streaks in it. She's one of those people who always look right. And she's easy to be with. She doesn't get prickly and hurt and bad-tempered. She doesn't fall out with people. She doesn't get into rages when Mum asks her about homework, or slam her door and knock her best pottery elephant off the shelf and smash it. Jennifer's always done her homework. Sheet after sheet of it, in her beautifully neat round handwriting, handed in on time. Her marks are always good enough, but not too good. Nobody calls Jennifer a keener.

And then there are Jennifer's clothes. Mum's always saying, 'I give each of you girls exactly the same clothes allowance. Can you please tell me, Kim, why you never have anything to wear?' Yes, Mum, I can tell you. Because I bought those jeans which would only have fitted me if I'd grown about four inches taller and four inches slimmer. Because I didn't read the care label on my new red top, which was the best thing I ever bought – even Jennifer wanted to borrow it. When it came out of the machine it was a sad red rag, and the two white towels I'd put in with it were sad pink rags. Mum made me pay for them, because they were new, so that was another twenty pounds, and now, surprise, surprise, I haven't got anything to wear. Jennifer doesn't spend much on clothes, but she always looks fantastic.

'Where did you get that skirt, Jennifer?'

'Oh, it was in the sale at River Island. It was only four ninety-nine. It was the last one.'

The last one. Of course.

Jennifer does gymnastics, and she's in the school netball team and the school tennis team. I love watching her play tennis. She seems to know just where the ball's going to go, and she's suddenly there with her racket, ready to hit it back. I asked her once how she did it, but she frowned and said, 'I don't know.' She doesn't even care about winning. If she loses she just shrugs and says, 'It was a nice game, anyway.'

But Jennifer hasn't been playing much tennis this summer. I wanted to book a court yesterday, but she said, 'Not today, Kim. I don't feel like it.' She lay sprawled on the grass, with a book beside her which she wasn't reading.

'Are you OK?' I asked. She nodded, and picked up the book and pretended to read it again. She didn't look that great. Later on I was playing CDs in my room when I heard Mum's voice. She sounded really angry. Angry? With Jennifer? I opened the door a crack, and listened.

'I don't ask you to do much, Jennifer, but I don't expect to come from work and find you haven't cleared the kitchen. You may be on holiday, but I'm not. I expect to have to chase after Kim when it's her turn, but not you.'

She was really shouting. I shut the door. I could feel a little secret grin curling over my face. A little later I heard Jennifer clattering the dishes, and the water gushing in the sink.

Things went on like that for a while. It was different from every other holiday. Jennifer didn't go out. When her friends rang she said she was busy. After a while they stopped ringing so much. She lay out on the grass day after day, with a book or a magazine or her Walkman. Sometimes she fell asleep for hours. It was so boring. When Mum came home she'd ask what we'd been doing and I'd say I'd been round to Katie's, or I'd been making chocolate brownies or whatever. Jennifer wouldn't say anything. She'd drift upstairs, looking as if she still had the sun in her eyes. Once I came out of the kitchen and I saw her standing halfway up the stairs, quite still, holding on to the banister and staring at nothing.

I thought it was going to go on for ever. Jennifer never asked what I was doing. I could have done anything I wanted, all those long, hot holidays. But suddenly everything changed. I'd been swimming with Katie and Lisa, but they were going off to have lunch at Burger King and I hadn't any money, so I came home alone. It was very hot and there was hardly anyone out on the streets. I went in through our back garden gate, and there was Jennifer as usual, sprawled on her back in the sun. But there was something about the way she was lying which was different. And her face looked wrong. It was a dirty-washing-up-water colour.

'Jennifer? *Jennifer*!' She didn't answer. She didn't move. I dropped my stuff on the grass and ran to her. My heart was banging and my fingers were sweaty. I had a horrible feeling that she wasn't ever going to answer. I bent down and shook her shoulder. Then her eyes opened and she looked at me.

'Are you OK? What's happened?'

'I feel funny. I think I fainted. Kim, get Mum.'

'Mum's at work.'

Jennifer tried to sit up. Her hair was dark with sweat and it stuck to her forehead. She looked awful, as if she was going to be sick.

'Kim, get Mum,' she said again, as if she hadn't understood what I said about Mum being at work.

'OK. I won't be a minute. Listen, just stay there, Jennifer, all right?' I ran across the grass to the kitchen door. If I used the kitchen phone I could still see Jennifer. She looked so bad. She looked . . .

'Mum! Mum, it's Jennifer . . .'

That was the beginning. After that it was like a tide coming in. You think you've got plenty of time, because the water's only up to your knees. Then you're thigh-deep, and the waves are pushing you hard. Suddenly the sea's all around you, and then between one wave and the next you lose your footing and when you reach down there's nothing, only deep, cold water. No matter how hard you struggle towards land, you can't get there again.

Everything changed. I remember the first time Mum took Jennifer to the doctor, that same evening because she still looked so awful.

'It's probably nothing, but we'll just get you checked

over.' And she must have phoned Dad, because he came home early too, and cooked fried chicken with rice and peas, and made a lot of jokes which didn't really hide the way either of us felt when surgery time was long over and Jennifer and Mum still didn't come back.

Jennifer was having tests. That's why they'd been so long. Mum looked pale, too.

'What kind of tests?' I asked Jennifer when Mum went upstairs to change.

'Oh. Blood and stuff. He looked at my legs.'

'Looked at your legs? What's wrong with your legs?'

'They've got all –' she paused, 'bruises on them.'

'Did somebody hit you? Is that what's wrong?'

Jennifer smiled, very faintly. 'Course not. They just came.'

She was wearing her white jeans. Suddenly I realised she'd been wearing jeans or a long cotton skirt for about two weeks. Never her shorts or her swimsuit, even though she was always lying in the sun.

'Show me.'

Jennifer hesitated. Then she took a quick look at the door to be sure it was shut, and unzipped her jeans. 'There.'

There were dark, splotchy bruises on her thighs. She looked down at them, then quickly at me. She looked almost . . . pleading. As if there was something she wanted me to say.

'They're not so bad,' I said. 'It was worse when you fell off your bike.'

'Yes,' said Jennifer quickly. 'Yes, it was, wasn't it.' And she did up her jeans again, looking relieved.

The next thing was that Jennifer had to go to hospital for more tests. The blood tests hadn't been too clear or something. Mum and Dad went too, but when they came back Jennifer wasn't with them.

'We dropped her off at Martina's,' said Mum. 'Peel some potatoes for me, would you, Kim?' She went out of the room and I heard her going upstairs, nearly as slowly as Jennifer had done. I peeled the potatoes, then I thought I'd go up and get my CD player so I could listen to music while I laid the table.

Mum's door was open. I just glanced in, the way you do. I wasn't trying to look or anything. Mum was lying on the bed, her face in her pillow. Dad was sitting beside her, with his arms round her as much as he could. They weren't saying anything, but Mum's back was shaking and I could tell she was crying. I went into my room really quickly and grabbed the CD player and went downstairs.

Jennifer came back very late and went straight to her room. I knocked and after a long time she said, 'Come in.' Then she looked at me and said, 'Oh. It's you.'

I fiddled with her light switch. 'Are you OK, Jennifer? I mean, were the tests all right and everything?'

Jennifer gave me the coldest, hardest look she had ever given me. 'Don't be stupid,' she said. I felt myself flush red all over, as if I'd done something wrong.

'How can the tests be OK,' went on Jennifer in the same voice, 'when they're to find out if I've got leukaemia and I'm probably going to die?'

Jennifer did have leukaemia. The test results came back and Mum and Dad told me. But it didn't mean Jennifer was going to die. The treatment for leukaemia was amazing these days. Most people recovered. I sat there while Mum and Dad told me all the hopeful things about leukaemia, and I thought of Mum lying on the bed crying, and I knew she'd guessed too, before the test results came back, just like Jennifer had.

It was a few weeks later that Mum came into my room when I was in bed, just before I fell asleep. I knew all sorts of other stuff by then, that I didn't want to know, about white cells counts and what was normal and what was Jennifer. Mum and Dad said they'd decided to be completely open with me. Jennifer was going to need a lot of treatment but it was going to work. She'd spent a lot of time in hospital already. The only thing Jennifer said was, 'If my hair falls out, I'm not going to wear a wig.' Then she wouldn't talk about any of it any more.

Mum sat on my bed and crossed her legs. It was nearly dark, but I could just about see her face looking at mine.

'Jennifer needs more treatment,' she said. 'Dr Aitchison's told us he thinks the best therapy for her at this stage is a bone marrow transplant.' That was the way Mum talked then, just like a doctor herself.

'A bone marrow transplant.'

'Yes. You see, if Jennifer could receive some healthy bone marrow which can make new cells for her, she'd have a good chance of making a complete recovery.'

'How can she? I mean, she can't have other people's bones transplanted.'

Mum sighed, as if I was being deliberately thick. And maybe I was. The whole thing was so horrible I didn't even want to understand it.

'Just the marrow,' she said. 'They can take it out of a healthy person's bones, and put it into Jennifer's.'

'How?' I asked faintly. Mum hesitated.

'The thing is,' she said, 'the bone marrow has to be a very close match to Jennifer's. It's no good just anybody being a donor, or her body will reject it. But people in a family are often a very close match. So Dad and I are going to be tested to see if we're good enough . . .' She was silent for a while, then she added, in a brisk voice as if she was asking me to do the washing-up, 'But the best chance of a match is from a sibling.'

A sibling. I heard the word as if it was just a word, then I understood. 'You mean – a sister?'

'Yes, Kim, there's a very good chance that your marrow might be a close enough match.'

My bone marrow! I felt completely sick. 'You mean – take out my bone marrow and give it to Jennifer?'

'Not all of it, don't be silly, Kim. Just a little bit.'

I notice what Mum doesn't say, as well as what she does. I noticed that she didn't say, *It won't hurt*.

'What do they do?'

'Well, they give you an anaesthetic of course, so it's just like going to sleep.'

'*What do they do, Mum*?'

'It's quite a simple operation. They just take some marrow from your bone – from your hip bone, it'd be – while you're asleep.'

'What with? A needle?'

'Well – yes. A sort of needle. Dr Aitchison said he'd be happy to talk it over with you, if you've got any questions.'

You bet I have, I thought, but I didn't say anything. I hate hospitals, I hate illness, I hate needles and above all I hate doctors explaining things to me as if I'm about two years old.

'It may not happen. You may not be a close enough match,' said Mum.

'No,' I said. 'After all, look how different we are. People are always saying we don't look like sisters.'

But we weren't as different as everybody thought. The tests

showed that Jennifer and I were more alike than anyone had ever believed. I saw Mum's face go shaky with relief, and Dad turned away and whistled through his teeth, because that was what he did when he couldn't handle us seeing how he felt. Then Mum and Dad were both looking at me. It was a strange, strange feeling. I wanted to say, *Take it away. Don't make it have to happen*. But I knew it was too late for that. Only Jennifer didn't react. She didn't look pleased or anything. She looked as if she was thinking about something else.

Jennifer had to have a lot of treatment to get her ready for the bone marrow transplant. She was in a little room on her own and I wasn't allowed to go in, because of infection getting to her. There was glass at the end wall and I used to wave to her and hold up little notes, but she didn't look terribly interested.

'She's very tired,' said Mum. 'It's the chemotherapy. Better leave her to rest now.' But I noticed that one time when Martina came with us, Jennifer sat right up on her bed and wrote little notes back to Martina. The next day she didn't want to see anyone, not even Mum.

'She's worried about her hair,' said Mum. Later on, in the car, I pulled my scrunchy off and my hair flopped round my face, as it always did. I tried to imagine what it would be like if it started falling out when I combed it. I tried to imagine a wig, but I couldn't.

But the next day Jennifer wouldn't see me again, and I stopped feeling sorry for her.

'She's such a bitch!' I said to Dad in the car on the way back. He didn't say anything.

'Why should I have holes in my bones and get my bone marrow sucked out, just for a bitch like her who won't even talk to me?'

I thought Dad would be angry with me, but he just met my eyes in the driving mirror. 'I can't give you a reason,' he said.

And now I'm in hospital. It's horrible. They've given me something which has dried up my mouth, and I haven't had anything to drink, and I'm really hungry. And there are people clattering about the whole time, and talking to me as if I'm an idiot. And I still haven't seen Jennifer.

And I'm frightened. I wonder if Jennifer's frightened too? She's waiting, all prepared, just as I am, so that as soon as they take my bone marrow it can go into her. And then, maybe, my healthy cells will take root in her and start to grow. After a while they won't be my cells any more; they'll be hers. They'll start making healthy blood for her, the way they should have done all along.

I can hear wheels skidding and squeaking on the lino. I know if I look up I'll see a trolley coming, and yet more people with J-cloth caps over their heads and big smiles on their faces. This time they haven't come to check me or chat to me. They've come to wheel me away.

I think of the bruises on Jennifer's legs. I think of her hair. Mum says she shuts her eyes when she combs her hair in the morning. Then she says she doesn't care, she isn't going to wear a wig anyway. People will just have to accept her the way she is. And Mum says, '*They will.*'

Just imagine, I'm a closer match to Jennifer than even Mum or Dad. But when you think of it, that's the way it ought to be. Your mum and dad get old and die, while you've still got a lot of your life left to live. But your sister doesn't die. She grows up, and goes to work, and maybe gets married, and has kids, and grows old, just the way you do. Your sister stays alive as long as you do, till you're two scrunched-up little old ladies together, laughing at the things you used to do when you were little. *Two old ladies*. Are you listening, Jennifer?

But it doesn't matter if you're listening or not. It doesn't even matter if you don't want to see me. We're as close a match as you can get, and there's nothing in the world either of us can do about it.

The Golden Gate

They opened the Golden Gate the summer of my twelfth birthday. Mum and Dad had already promised we'd go to Mere Park for my birthday treat. Everyone was talking about the Golden Gate. It was amazing, they said. First of all there was the Death Slide, sheer as the side of a house and shiny as a waterfall, then you shot straight into the Golden Gate with its massive twisted bars and sheets of blinding metal. The Golden Gate was always shut. You smashed straight into it. One by one hundreds of screaming kids plunged from the top of the Death Slide, hurtled down the precipice and crashed into the Golden Gate. Except that they didn't really crash.

The Gate was a miracle of advanced laser technology, it said in the TV adverts for Mere Park. *An unbelievable, inimitable phenomenon of fear*. Nothing like it had ever been seen before anywhere in the world. The Gate looked solid and three-dimensional, barring your way as you raced towards it at thirty miles an hour. Maybe more. I couldn't wait to go on the Golden Gate. I wondered if I'd scream and hide my eyes the way kids did on the advert. It was the kind of screaming where fear and pleasure are so mixed up no one can tell which is which – not even the kid who's screaming.

There were stories about the couple who'd invented the Golden Gate. They were called the Damianos. Virgil and Bella Damiano. Virgil was short and fat and he always wore a suit no matter how hot it was. Bella Damiano was tall, and she wore brilliant blue leggings with stars on them. Real silver stars, people said. And a sun and moon of pure gold on her baggy sky-blue T-shirt. They weren't Mere Park staff. People said the owners of Mere Park had offered them a fortune to set up the Golden Gate there. Others said that the Damianos had refused to take a penny. Then there was the story that sometimes the Damianos would pick out a kid from the queue for a Mystery Ride. No one knew how that kid got chosen and it didn't happen often. The kid would never say afterwards what the Mystery Ride was like. Of course everyone wanted to be chosen. Bella Damiano walked up and down the queue of kids, her glance flicking over faces and then away. Suddenly she'd stop, bend down, draw a kid aside. No one else ever heard what she said.

There weren't any little kids in the queue for the Golden Gate when we arrived. The Gate was just too real and dangerous and powerful. Most of the queue were my age, or older. As I joined the queue I saw it was going to be a long wait. I didn't mind. We'd got to Mere Park early, and the sky was a clear pale blue. It was going to be hot. Mum and Dad had promised we could stay until Mere Park closed, so we had all day. A long, hot summer day with my birthday picnic and the chocolate fudge birthday cake Dad had made. In the afternoon we were going to take a boat out on the lake, and on the way home we'd stop for chicken and chips at the service station. I was slowly shuffling forward, thinking of all this, when my sister Pearl tugged my arm.

'David. Let me in.'

I moved to one side so Pearl could get into the queue beside me. Then I said, 'What are you doing here, Pearl? This ride isn't for little kids. It's really scary.'

Pearl smiled confidently. 'I'll be OK, David,' she said.

I had to smile back. Pearl is tough. Because she had long blonde hair and she's only five, lots of grown-ups think she's quite sweet, but that's because they haven't seen her flying down the lane behind our house on her bike, screeching, 'Out of my way!' and scattering everyone in front of her. Mum knows what Pearl gets up to, but she tries not to stop her doing things. Once I heard Mum say to Dad, 'It's so hard to let them have their freedom. After Rob . . .'

Dad said, 'I know. But we've got to.'

My brother Rob was killed two years ago, just before Christmas. Rob was coming home from a rehearsal: he was playing guitar for the school musical. He was on a crossing, but the car didn't stop. The driver cried in court and said he didn't even see Rob. He'd been drinking at an office Christmas party at lunch-time, and he was driving home. Lots of my friends think I don't mind about Rob any more. They think I've forgotten him, because I don't talk about him. But I haven't. I always carry his photograph in my pocket. It's really battered now from going everywhere with me for two years. I don't think Mum and Dad know I take Rob's photograph everywhere, but Pearl does, because sometimes she asks me if she can look at it. Pearl remembers Rob really well, even though she was only three when he died, because Rob was always building things for her out of Duplo and taking her out on her trike.

'It'll be your turn soon, Davey,' said Pearl. I jumped. I'd been a million miles away. Then I saw that Bella Damiano was walking towards us. I knew her at once. Sky-blue T-shirt with silver stars and golden sun and moon. Yes, they were real gold and silver all right. And her dark fierce face was real, too. She was looking at us intently, then she came towards us. I felt a flush of excitement go up in my face, but she folded her legs up like an acrobat, squatted down by Pearl and whispered something in Pearl's ear. I couldn't hear what it was. Pearl whispered something back. Bella Damiano frowned, and looked up at me.

'You're David,' she said. I nodded.

'I can't take you on the Mystery Ride,' she said, 'I can

only take Pearl. You're carrying too much with you.'

'No, I'm not!' I said indignantly. I'd left my rucksack at the picnic place. I wasn't carrying anything. It was just a pathetic excuse.

'I'm sorry,' said Bella Damiano, 'not this time.' She took Pearl's hand. As she led Pearl to the front of the queue Bella Damiano brushed against me. Then she and Pearl disappeared into the entrance.

'Wait for me at the bottom, Pearl!' I yelled after her.

It wasn't long before my turn came. Just an ordinary ride, not a Mystery Ride, but that was exciting enough. When I got to the top I looked down and for a second I didn't think I could let go. My mind was telling me that those massive golden bars were made of light, but my body didn't believe it. You had to lie down flat, then you'd shoot over the lip of the slide. You'd see the Golden Gate coming at you. Then a kid behind me grumbled, 'Make your mind up,' and I had to let go.

There was a slow second as I slid over the top, then a rushing current of speed grabbed hold of me and tore me away. I screamed and covered my eyes as the great metal gates lunged at me. My screams joined thousands of others then I was through, on the other side, coasting to a stop in the dark padded safety area. Virgil Damiano was there to make sure everyone got off the ride quickly. Outside, waiting for me, was Pearl.

'Did you like your Mystery Ride, Pearl?' I asked her. Her face glowed like the Golden Gate itself. Then she said,

'It was great. But it wasn't my proper Mystery Ride. Bella said that wasn't ready yet.'

Virgil Damiano lounged out of the safety area. He bowed to Pearl. 'Your Mystery Ride is prepared,' he announced.

Pearl grabbed my hand. We went back to the queue and Bella waved us both to the front. The other kids didn't seem to mind. Everyone knew about Mystery Rides, and hoped they'd get one themselves one day. We climbed up to the top and Pearl lay down, smiling as if she knew something wonderful was going to happen. She looked so small lying there that I felt a sudden pang of fear.

'You don't have to go down, Pearl, if you don't want to,' I whispered. But she moved into position, and in a second the Death Slide whizzed her away from me and she disappeared through the Golden Gate. Then it was my turn. It wasn't so frightening the second time. The Golden Gate loomed, solid and terrifying, then it just – *disappeared*. I got off at the end of the ride, brushed off my jeans and went out to find Pearl.

She wasn't there. At first I thought she was so eager for her next ride that she'd joined the queue again. But she hadn't. I went back inside. Virgil Damiano had gone and there was a young helper I hadn't seen before in his place.

'Have you seen a little blonde girl come down?' I asked.

He shook his head. I looked round outside again. Lots of little kids everywhere. No Pearl. Perhaps she'd gone back to the queue. I'd ask Bella Damiano. But there was no Bella, and no Pearl, only a red-headed girl helper. I asked her where the Damianos were, and she said, 'There's a fault in the Gate. They're just fixing it.'

Perhaps Pearl had gone back to Mum and Dad? But it wasn't like Pearl to go off without telling me. Fear nagged in my head like a bad tooth as I ran back to the tree where Mum and Dad were spreading out my birthday picnic. Mum looked up and smiled.

'Hello, love. Had a good time? Where's Pearl?'

'I don't know. She went off. I thought she'd be here.'

Mum's hands went still, holding the picnic plates. Dad got up from the rug.

'OK,' said Mum calmly, 'I'll stay here in case she comes back. Davey, go and look again by the Golden Gate. You might have missed her. Nick –'

But Dad had already gone, looking for Pearl.

She wasn't at the Golden Gate. I began to run. I blundered past people taking Camcorder shots of their kids, I trampled the edges of other people's picnics, I brushed past grinning kids licking their ice creams. A man shouted, 'Watch where you're going!'

The bright perfect day was turning into a nightmare, and everyone else was still smiling. The ecstatic screams of kids going down the Golden Gate echoed like screams on TV war bulletins. I'd lost Pearl.

Mum was talking to a security man by the time I got back to our rug.

'She wasn't there,' I panted, and the man spoke into his mobile. Minutes were passing, and no Pearl. The man started to tell Mum how many kids went missing each day, and how they always turned up. Mum nodded, but she was pale. I looked at my chocolate fudge cake with its twelve candles. They were stuck in crooked, because Pearl had helped. I felt sick.

'I'll go back to the Golden Gate,' I said desperately.

'No need. They've checked it twice already,' said the security man.

But I had to do something. I ran, and as I ran my hand went automatically to my pocket as it always did when I was tired or sad or in trouble, just to feel the outline of Rob's photograph. My fingers groped in disbelief. Nothing. The photograph had gone. First Pearl, now Rob. When had I lost it? I'd never find it with all these people. It'd be trampled underfoot. I'd *got* to get it back – I hadn't got a copy. Frantically, I started to search. There it was! I pounced on a square of white paper bowling over the grass in the breeze. My fingers trembled as I turned it over, but I knew already it wasn't the photograph. It was just picnic rubbish.

I was bending down to look again when I remembered

Pearl. It seemed as if I felt her hand, reaching for mine. But I had to get my photograph back! I couldn't just let it go, could I? I stood still. I felt as if I was being torn in half, then suddenly I knew what to do, just as if someone was telling me. Pearl was alone, and she'd be frightened. Rob wouldn't want her to be frightened. She was more important than my photograph. I couldn't waste time looking for it now.

What I did next may sound strange to you, but at the time it seemed like the only thing I could do. I queued, and I went back up to the top of the Golden Gate. I had a feeling that if I found Pearl anywhere, it would be there. I lay on my back at the top, and began to move. I stared straight at the Golden Gate until it shivered into splinters of light all around me, and I was through. And there was Pearl. Breathless as if she'd just come down the ride, though I knew she hadn't. There'd been no one else at the top, and she hadn't been in the queue in front of me. Virgil Damiano lifted her off the slide.

'Where've you been?' I asked her. 'Everyone's looking for you.'

She looked at me. There's a word for how Pearl looked. Radiant.

'I've been through the Golden Gate,' she said. 'I saw Rob.'

A shiver went through me like a cold wind. 'Pearl! You didn't! You can't have!'

'I did. I did see Rob. You can see him too, if you want.'

She took my hand, not like a little kid but as if she was guiding me, and she led me back to the queue. There was Bella Damiano, back again, and again she nodded us through to the front. I knew I ought to go and tell Mum and Dad I'd found Pearl. But something pulled me like a magnet. *Rob.* Could it be true? Could I really see him? Then we were at the top.

'Look. Look through the Gate,' said Pearl. I looked down. There was the Golden Gate, beautiful and terrifying, and there, on the other side – was it? Could it be? A boy in jeans torn at the knees, and a T-shirt, and an LA Raiders cap pulled on backwards. Rob. Looking just exactly as he'd looked in my photograph, smiling at us.

'Rob,' I whispered.

'Come on,' said Pearl. 'If we go through the Golden Gate now we'll be with Rob. You can go first this time.'

My knees trembled as I lay down. Rob. Rob was there. I was going to him. I hadn't lost him, even though I'd lost his photograph. Photograph. My whole body went stiff. What had Dad said about the Golden Gate, when he was trying to explain how it worked to Pearl?

'It's a bit like a photograph, only it's not flat. It's in three dimensions, just like you are, so it looks real. And it can move.'

A bit like a photograph. But in three dimensions. No

wonder it looked like my photograph. I remembered Bella Damiano brushing against me. She'd been as quick as a pickpocket. So that was where my photograph had gone. Those Damianos had taken it to make a three-dimensional image of Rob out of laser light. But why? I looked down. There was Rob, sunlight on his hair, looking at me, smiling from the other side of the Golden Gate. Surely it couldn't hurt to let go? Then another picture came into my mind. Mum's hands tight on the picnic plates. Those lines suddenly deep on Dad's forehead. The crooked candles. They'd trusted me to find Pearl. What if we both disappeared? I hesitated. Half of me longed to dive through the Golden Gate to where Rob stood. But I saw Mum and Dad, alone under the tree with my birthday cake.

'Pearl,' I said, 'I'm dizzy. Let's go back down.'

As we turned to leave I took my last look at the Golden Gate, and Rob. I knew I could never come here again. Rob was still smiling, just as he'd been smiling on that long-ago sunny day when I took the photograph with my new camera. It was a smile of summer and good times. Was it a trick of laser light, or was it Rob, our Rob? I'd never know.

Bella Damiano was at the bottom of the steps when we got down. She looked at me hard, then she said, 'So you had your Mystery Ride after all, David.'

'I didn't go down,' I answered.

Bella Damiano smiled at me and her fierce face was

suddenly gentle. Then I noticed a battered square of paper in her hand. I knew what it was, but I didn't ask her to give it back. I knew I didn't need it any more.

I never told Mum and Dad how I had found Pearl. When I lit the crooked candles on my chocolate fudge cake and they all sang HAPPY BIRTHDAY I thought of Rob. I knew he wasn't waiting for us behind the Golden Gate, in the laser image the Damianos had made. He wasn't on the tattered square of that photograph I'd carried around for two years, either. If he was anywhere, he was here with us.